Send not to know

The Cold War is coming to an end, as the Soviet Union holds free elections and the Berlin Wall is breached. Dan Leyland is chairing a conference of European NGOs in Perugia, and he observes that some of his colleagues are unhappy about having their political illusions shattered. He gets to know an Italian contessa who is acting as an interpreter, and when she confides in him about her troubled marriage he glimpses the possibility that his own post-marital loneliness could be coming to an end. But events do not always work out as expected – neither in politics nor in personal relationships.

This volume is the third in *The Peacekeepers* trilogy; and when Dan talks with his parents and their group of friends, whose lives were completely disrupted by events in 'far away countries' in the 1930s, they tell him of their hopes and fears for a better future. The action moves from London to Switzerland, Germany and Italy, and back to London. Some of the events are predictable and others are not.

No man is an island,
Entire of itself.
Each is a piece of the continent,
A part of the main.
If a clod be washed away by the sea,
Europe is the less.
As well as if a promontory were.
As well as if a manor of thine own
Or of thine friend's were.
Each man's death diminishes me,
For I am involved in mankind.
Therefore, send not to know
For whom the bell tolls,
It tolls for thee.

John Donne, 1624

Send not to know

to know

Derek Walker

To Eileen,

with every good wish

Derek Walker

ISBN 978-0-9561569-5-2

Typesetting and design by Christine Price

Published 2016 by Derek Walker,
Dorset Square, London NW1

Distribution at www.lulu.com

ABOUT THE AUTHOR

DEREK WALKER grew up in Northern Ireland and was educated at Portadown College. He graduated at the London School of Economics, majoring in International Relations, and since then he has continued to live in London. For ten years he worked as a journalist, latterly as Deputy Editor of the *British Weekly*. In 1966 he became Education Officer of the newly-formed Voluntary Committee on Overseas Aid and Development. When VCOAD was dissolved in 1977 he became Director of the Centre for World Development Education (later renamed Worldaware) which took over its educational work. For ten years he chaired the European Development Education Curriculum Network (EDECN). In 1997 he was appointed OBE. Since retiring from Worldaware he has published eight novels (see end pages).

CHAPTER ONE 30 March, 1989

Dan experienced a sense of relief when the formal proceedings for opening the conference came to an end. He was well used to chairing international events but he realized that this introductory session was actually a public relations exercise for their Italian hosts. They had invited along the local television station and various dignitaries, including the mayor of Perugia, the bishop and the head of the Carabinieri in his full-dress uniform.

The mayor in his welcoming address had been a little confused about the purpose of the conference, assuming that because the participants were representatives of organizations involved with international development they must be going to talk about how to raise money. So, in his response Dan had tried to explain that the assembled members of the Development Awareness Network for the European Community were people charged with the more complex task of raising – in a variety of ways – awareness of the interdependence between rich countries and those that were euphemistically described as 'developing'. He wondered how the translators, especially the young man working for the local television company, had coped with his attempt to use simple words to explain a complicated process. Before the meeting began he had spent some time with the translators, knowing the difficulties that technical terms were bound to pose for them.

Now, as he moved from the lecture hall to the brightly-lit room of the university in which the drinks reception was being held, he reflected that the next three days should be an easier task, since the people whose discussions he would be chairing were already familiar with the questions, even though they might differ widely about the answers. A Danish participant, Kirsten, approached him as he made his way to the buffet. "I thought you handled that well. I'm not sure the Italian big noises knew why they were here," she said, patting his shoulder affectionately.

He noticed that she moved on purposefully in the direction of Jaume, one of the Spanish participants, and remembered that their two organizations had been involved in a joint educational project which, according to rumour, had involved a great deal of travel between Barcelona and Copenhagen.

Next to accost him was Franco, the Italian member of the conference organizing committee. "I thought that went quite well," he said. "It's the first time we have been able to get a mention on television about the work we are doing in Italy."

"You must have worked hard to persuade so many important people to attend," said Dan.

"It helps when they hear that the EC is supporting us. In Italy people are very happy to be involved with European organizations.

"I think you know that Brussels is paying for simultaneous translation only at the plenary sessions," he went on. "So we have recruited a few volunteer interpreters to help with the group discussions. I must introduce you to the Italian volunteer. She is able to help with both English and French translation. I think she is over there in the corner – if we can get through the crowd."

As they began to make their way through the chattering throng towards the far end of the room Franco lowered his voice to a note of confidentiality. "I am wondering whether this lady might actually have been given the job of reporting back on us to government sources. As you can guess, some of the organizations in our delegation have political agendas of their own that are – how do you say it? – 'a bit way out'. Her husband is a Christian Democrat politician, and it was one of the church-based NGOs that offered us her services. She has been a teacher of English and French, I think. But either we are being paranoid or they are. There is nothing happening here that we have to hide. By the way, she wants us to call her Gina, but she is actually the Contessa Urbisaglia."

Dan was expecting to meet an imperious lady with patrician features, clad in the latest creation from a fashion house in Milan. To his surprise he was introduced to a young-looking woman, casually dressed in checked blue shirt and jeans, with light brown, curly hair and a squarish, fresh-complexioned face that reminded him of women he had encountered in Switzerland, Austria and Bavaria. Her voice was soft, with the merest hint of an accent, and he quickly realized that she was well accustomed to speaking English.

Franco left them together as he went off to perform his duty as host to the mayor and the bishop, and Dan quickly found himself engaged in a relaxed and friendly conversation. It was the first time she had been involved in an event of this kind, she said, and she was finding the mix of different kinds of people, different nationalities and different organizations quite fascinating. What kind of organization did he work for?

"I'm director of a small NGO called CPEEE – the Council for Promoting Enterprise in Emerging Economies," he replied. "It was the brainchild of a man who made a fortune setting up companies that organize supply chains for businesses in Africa and South-East Asia. A charitable trust that he established provides the bulk of our funding; and in spite of the name most of our activities are in the UK – persuading multinationals, and others, to foster entrepreneurship in developing countries where they have a presence."

"It sounds like a very specialized kind of work," said Gina.

"Yes, I suppose it does. We also work with the media, trying to get them to understand better the contribution that private enterprise can make to development."

She smiled, and he was instantly attracted by the warmth and humour in the sparkling of her brown eyes. "I think your work might not make you popular with a lot of our colleagues here today," she said. "If development NGOs in other countries are like the ones in Italy then a lot of them seem to think that private enterprise is the enemy of development, not its friend."

"You're right: they do. A lot of them were founded in the '50s and '60s and they're still living in the past. In spite of all the evidence contradicting the sacred Marxist dogma they still want to stick with the dogma, even if they prefer to call it by other names – like 'dependency theory' or even 'liberation theology'. I expect we'll be hearing some of it tomorrow."

She laughed – a throaty, conspiratorial chuckle. "I've had to listen to quite a lot of that. The organization I help as a volunteer does some marvellous work with mothers and children mainly in refugee camps, and the people who do that work are very practical about finding ways to achieve a lot with a small amount of money. But we also have people who work in the department that does educational programmes in Italy, and they are not happy because we have not mounted political campaigns attacking our government and the companies that trade with the Third World. They sometimes have big arguments with the people who raise money from the public to fund the organization's work, and also with our governing council, where there is one bishop who often gives them support."

"That sounds very like the picture in several British NGOs that I've had contact with," said Dan. "People get involved with working for international development from a whole range of different motives. I suppose that's inevitable, since there are so many different ways of approaching it."

Gina nodded, and hesitated for a moment before speaking again. "I am… a little surprised that they made you the chairman of DANEC, when there is so much hostility to business, even among people who don't take the Marxist line."

Dan smiled and replied, "I think one reason might be that my organization is very small and doesn't look important enough to be a threat to anyone. And just because of its particular specialism it is not in direct competition with any of the others; so I suppose I looked like somebody who could be impartial – especially since I didn't ask for the job. But actually, like a lot of decisions made by committees, it may have owed more to accident than to design. I happened to be someone who was available and willing, if a little reluctant, at the time when they were looking for a chairman."

"Do you think that attitudes to Marxist solutions for the world's problems will start to change now, after what's been happening in Russia – like Yeltsin winning the election yesterday?" she asked.

"My guess is that like all religions – and the Marxist faith is a sort of religion – it has two kinds of believers. Those who are still capable of rational thought will see the error of their ways now and move on, as a lot of them have been doing ever since Khrushchev admitted to the faithful a few facts about Stalin that the rest of us had been convinced of for a long time. The second kind, whose faith has its origins in some deep emotional need, will find excuses for hanging on to it. Their favourite explanation seems to be that the wonderful procedure for creating heaven on earth was hijacked by a wicked individual who misused it for his own evil ends. They refuse to see that it wasn't the tyrant who produced the system but the system that produced the tyrant."

"That is an interesting way to explain it," said Gina. "I think there are a lot of people in Italy who are adopting that point of view. But you will think that I am – what is the English expression? – a 'political animal', but really I am not. My husband is in politics but I... don't get involved with that activity. I am just annoyed when people bring their politics into all kinds of other activities and it prevents them from making sensible decisions."

"Do you think that might be because their politics has a kind of religious dimension for them, affecting everything they do?" he asked.

"I don't know. I think in Italy it is too easy to use politics to get the things you want – a job for your daughter, a contract to build a bridge, a professorship in the university. People tell lies to themselves about the reasons why they do things, and then they really believe their own lies. Do you think I am being a cynic?"

"I think you are looking very realistically at how things actually happen, and that's not always easy to do if you're working inside an organization that's committed to a particular ideology."

"Is your organization one that is committed to an ideology?" she asked.

"I would say that it isn't; but I think one or two of my Council members believe we should be dedicated to promoting the virtues of capitalism. My own view is that capitalism – to borrow from Churchill's comment on democracy – is the least bad of all the economic systems that have so far evolved. But it's not so much the system that matters as the way in which it is applied."

"Rather like lipstick, maybe?" she queried, directing his eyes with a slight inclination of her head to the face of a young woman standing a couple of yards away whose scarlet lips were in violent discord with the orange tint of her hair.

"Yes, indeed. An apt comparison," he replied with a smile. Then, suppressing the fear that he might sound patronizing, he said, "May I ask where you learned to speak such excellent English?"

"I was fortunate enough to have a very good teacher in school. She had married a British soldier who was stationed in Bassano at the end of the War and who decided to come back and live in Italy when he left the army. I think he must have been very much in love with her. I met him a few times in my last year at school, when I visited her house to borrow books. And then I had four months in London, at Bedford College, when I was studying for my degree. That helped me to get my accent right, I think, because I didn't lose it when I spent a postgraduate year at Harvard. That was on a scholarship, of course. My parents didn't have money but I was lucky enough to be good at passing examinations."

"That's very interesting. My mother spent a few months at Harvard when she was student. That was in the Thirties. My mother is Spanish."

"Spanish? Oh, now I understand," she exclaimed. "When I first saw you going up to the platform before the meeting began I thought you must be one of the Italian group that I hadn't been introduced to. You don't look English, even though you sound English. Oh dear, I hope you don't think I'm being rude."

He shook his head. "Of course not. I know exactly what you mean. I have a sister who has blonde hair and looks very English – much more like my father."

"Have you spent much time in Spain?" she asked.

"I've been there only twice – after the death of Franco. My mother has been only once, to see to my grandfather's grave. He was killed by the Falangists, even though he wasn't a combatant. And my grandmother's brother was killed by the Communists, because he was a Catholic priest."

"They were terrible times," said Gina. "My husband's father fought on Franco's side, with the so-called 'volunteers' from Italy. In reality they were just detachments from the Italian Army. He said he wasn't a Fascist but he was opposed to the Communists, and Mussolini's propaganda made them

6

out to be the dominant force on the Spanish government side. Was your father in Spain when he met your mother?"

"No. She came to Britain as a refugee after her father's death. But I have an uncle who fought in the International Brigade. He's not actually a family member, but I grew up calling him 'Uncle Roddy' because he's been a friend of my parents since before the War."

"Do you feel that you're partly Spanish?" she asked.

"Not really. Spain was still a dictatorship when I was growing up. And I think my mother was concentrating on becoming British. She didn't have any close family left in Spain. Her mother had died in childbirth when she was quite young. But I did learn to speak Spanish – I suppose because it was too good an opportunity to miss, having someone at home to tutor me. And I think my mother was pleased because I grew up to look like my Spanish grandfather."

"He must have been a handsome man," said Gina, smiling.

It had been a long time since anyone had complimented Dan on his looks, but it had happened often enough in the past for him to accept Gina's comment as a compliment that was sincere.

"Well, my mother was – still is, in my opinion – a very beautiful woman; and my father's not bad looking either. So I've been very lucky with my genes," he replied. Over her shoulder he saw the DANEC Joint Secretaries, Fred Winter and Kurt Halder, making their way towards him.

"I think I'm about to become involved in official business again," he said, "but I'd love to be able to have a proper conversation. Is there any possibility you would join me for dinner tomorrow evening? I noticed from the agenda that they have left the evening free as a breathing space from conference activities."

A little to his surprise, for he was very uncertain what her reaction would be to his impulsive invitation, her eyes lit up with pleasure. "Oh, I would love to do that. I don't really know anyone else here, and I have enjoyed talking to you."

"I'll look forward to it," he said. "Some time tomorrow I'll speak to you about where to meet. I happen to know a good restaurant for a leisurely conversation because I stayed in Perugia a few years ago, on holiday."

As Fred and Kurt arrived she said, "I'll leave you to your official business," and moved quietly away.

"Who's the beautiful woman?" Fred asked.

"The unofficial Italian translator, the Contessa Urbisaglia – I think I've got that right," he replied. "Do we have a problem? Has the bishop decided to excommunicate us? You look worried."

"Not a serious problem, and we think you will find a solution," said Kurt. "One of the Belgians, Yves Guillaume, has handed us a resolution which he wants to move at the plenary session tomorrow morning." He held up a typewritten A4 sheet of paper. "It's in French – he's a Walloon – but I will translate."

Kurt read slowly and hesitantly from the paper: "This conference resolves to urge President Gorbachev not to deviate from socialist economic policy and to maintain Soviet support for Third World governments which are committed to the Marxist vision of liberation for their peoples."

"Remarkable brevity for a resolution coming from that political sector," said Dan. "I assume he has lined up at least one supporter to second it."

"Oh yes. René Maillot, one of the French gang of '68, has put his name to it," said Fred. "They're all very unhappy about what's been happening in Moscow."

"It must be very unsettling when your Promised Land is finally proved to be a mirage," said Dan. "But there seems to be a hard core of true believers who want to go on urging us to keep travelling in that direction. It's always hard to admit that you've made a mistake, but for most of us it's part of the process of growing up. Anyhow, we must decide what to do about this resolution."

"I don't think there's any chance it would get passed by the plenary, but the fact that we debated it would give ammunition to the people in Brussels who think DANEC is a waste of money," said Fred.

"I think what we need is for someone to propose from the floor that Monsieur Guillaume's resolution is not appropriate business for the plenary, and I will then immediately put that procedural resolution to the meeting," said Dan. "And I trust that some discreet lobbying by you two will make sure it's passed by a comfortable majority. That will mean that, although the resolution will be circulated with the agenda papers, it will appear in the minutes only as a resolution by Monsieur Yves Guillaume' – and not at all in the conference report."

"Spot on," said Fred. "Who would be the best person to propose the procedural resolution?"

Dan pondered for a moment. "I think we ought to avoid the risk of knee-jerk reactions of the kind we've sometimes seen in the past. You know, the kind that are based on perceptions which are completely irrelevant but emotionally very appealing. So the mover of the resolution should be from one of the smaller countries, and preferably a woman."

"What about Aisling Maguire?" Fred suggested. "She's a sensible woman who would understand immediately what's at stake. And the Irish group are well thought of."

"A good choice," said Dan. "If you like I'll have a word with her. Who can we ask to second the resolution?"

"It might be a good idea to involve Franco Benigni," said Kurt. "I know the Italian group are deeply divided, but I'm sure a majority of them would follow his lead; and they are the largest group. Should Fred and I talk to him?"

"Do that," said Dan. "If it all goes to plan we can finalize the details back at the hotel tonight before we turn in."

CHAPTER TWO 31 March, 1989

As they settled at the table to which they had been led by an elderly, white-haired waiter whose face was familiar to Dan from previous visits he noticed a cordon bleu certificate hanging on the wall. "That's reassuring," he remarked, "but I'm even more reassured by the fact that there's no carpet on the floor. I think the best meals I've had have all been in restaurants without carpets. It seems illogical, but I expect there's some rational explanation."

Gina responded with the throaty chuckle that had attracted him on the previous day. "It probably means they prefer to spend money on the kitchen rather than in the dining-room," she said. "I feel comfortable here already. I think the owners know they don't have to pretend to be something that they are not."

When they had studied the menu and given their order, for lasagne with mushrooms and truffles, followed by ossobuco, Gina said, "I thought you dealt well with that silly resolution this morning. Was the intervention by the sensible Irish woman something you had pre-arranged?"

"Yes. That's not the kind of thing you can leave to chance."

"I've seen a lot of problems created when well-meaning people too innocent for their own good weren't able to appreciate just how devious some political activists can be," she said. "Because I've not been actively engaged myself I think I may sometimes have been in a better position to observe the way they were manoeuvring – often to gain quite trivial objectives. I'm talking about the charity that I work for, not about a political party."

"Did you ever get involved with any of your husband's political activities?" he asked; and as he asked the question he realized that his motive was actually to find out more about her marriage.

"Actually I did in the early days. I suppose it was one of the reasons why he married me." She gave a little twisted smile that added fuel to his interest. "At that time he was standing for parliament, and there's a theory that it's helpful for a rising politician to have a... a presentable wife. But he lost his seat in the '83 election and since then... well, public appearances

10

have not been so important. He moves in more rarefied circles, and it isn't the public that he has to impress."

"Where do you live?" Dan asked.

"In Rome. After we were married we had a small flat for about three years in the suburb called EUR. The architecture is horrible, but there are lots of museums. Then, after my son Bruno was born we were able to afford a house in Aventino, not very far from the UN Food and Agriculture Organization. I expect you've been there. At that time Guido had some early success in business. You remember the great inflation that happened in the Seventies? For some reason it worked to his advantage. And, of course, his political contacts were helpful to his business. I think they are in most countries, but they seem to be specially useful in Italy." There was an acerbic note in her voice.

"Did you grow up in Rome?" he asked.

"No. I was born in Bassano. It's a small town to the north of Venice."

"I visited it a couple of years ago," he said, "when I was holidaying in Venice just after Christmas. I wanted to see the pictures by the two artists called 'Bassano' that hang in the Civic Museum. I remember there was an extraordinary Nativity tableau on a raft moored in the river, beside the bridge."

"My family home is just beyond the bridge, in Angarano, the part of town across the river from the walled city. My father, who came from a farming family, opened a little grocery shop there, and my brother owns it now."

Seeing the look of surprise on his face she said, "I haven't always been a contessa, you know. After university in Venice and Harvard I got a job teaching English in a school in Rome. One of my student friends who had become an interpreter asked me to help her one weekend at a conference. It was a little like this conference, with several smaller discussion groups, and so they needed extra interpreters. That was when I met Guido."

"So you were still quite young then?"

"I was twenty-two. I think you might describe it as a 'whirlwind romance': tall, handsome young aristocrat – though not rich at that time, so no red Ferrari – meets impressionable peasant girl (with a university degree) and sweeps her off her feet. Guido's mama disapproved of me, of course, and I think that getting married to me was his way of demonstrating his independence."

"I can think of other reasons why he might have been impatient to get married," said Dan. And at that moment their first course arrived. As they ate it she asked him about some of the organizations represented at the conference, and made some perceptive comments on the individuals taking part.

As the waiter came to clear away their plates she asked, "How did you come to involve yourself in this kind of activity?"

"I suppose my interest was awakened quite early in life," he replied. "My father was a Labour Member of Parliament for about six years after the War, and he and my mother and their friends used to talk a lot about politics, especially international affairs. One of their close friends – I called him Uncle Daniel, and I was actually named after him – had been involved, in a minor role, in the setting up of the UN and of NATO. Later, after he'd taken part in the Korean War, he became an academic and wrote books about political and military history. I admired him, and when I was growing up I talked a lot with him and his wife, Aunty Ruth, who writes novels. One of them, I know, has been translated into Italian."

"What is that book about?" she asked.

"It's about the adventures of two young people, an English woman and a German man, in 1848."

"The year of revolutions – is she a romantic?"

"No. I would say she's an anti-romantic. The background to her story reveals a lot about the reasons why the revolutionaries failed to achieve their objectives, and in most places made things worse than they had been before. Ruth actually had quite a lot of influence on me when I was a teenager. You know how it is – even though you have a good relationship with your parents, as I did, there are things you find it easier to talk about to someone else who isn't a member of the family. I used to share some of my teenage idealism with her and she, very tactfully, encouraged me to temper it with realism. Years later, when my marriage broke up she was the person who helped me to work out what I ought to do."

"Are you divorced, then?" she asked, and he thought he detected a note of genuine interest in her voice.

"Yes, about nine years ago. I suppose it was a classic example of two people getting married before they were really ready for it. We met when we were both doing a year's VSO assignment in St Lucia. That's Voluntary Service Overseas. Happily they don't do those short postgraduate assignments anymore. They were usually great fun for the young volunteers but often not very useful for their hosts. But I digress. We were caught up in a romantic encounter and impatient to be married when we got home to Britain. However, before we'd had time to really get to know each other I took a job with the Economist Intelligence Unit that involved a lot of travel away from home. I didn't realize I was neglecting Catherine until it was too late, and somebody else had begun to take my place in her life. I tried to sort it out, but without success, and so we got divorced."

"You are so lucky in England to be able to get divorced without a lot of difficulties," said Gina, speaking with an intensity that intrigued him.

"That's only been the case for less than twenty years," he said. "In fact, the Matrimonial Causes Act, that made the law more civilized, was passed just the year before we got married."

"Are you still... on your own?" she asked. And at that point their second course arrived – ossobucuo with risotto, and spinach.

"Yes, I haven't met anyone who wanted to take me on," he replied when the waiter had departed.

"I'm sorry, I shouldn't have been asking you such intimate questions," she said; but she didn't look penitent.

"Why not? We're usually more reluctant to talk about intimate matters with the people that we're closest to. Strangers don't bring a previous agenda to the table," he replied.

"That is so true; but sometimes people who are not close to you have their own agendas, too. I am thinking of the people I have to mix with in Rome. Everyone is connected to someone else, who is maybe in politics, or in a newspaper. You make a casual remark and the next day it is being talked about and twisted by people who don't even know you."

"You sound as if you've had some bad experiences," he said.

"Just one or two. I very quickly learned to be careful."

They both addressed the food with enthusiasm, and for a few minutes there was silence, apart from the buzz of other people's conversation in the background.

When he had extracted the last drop of mouth-watering marrow Dan asked, "Have you had a look in the wonderful Sala di Udienza, or haven't you had any time for sight-seeing?"

"I haven't been there this time," she replied, "but I did come to Perugia about two years ago for the sole purpose of seeing the sights. I was going through a phase where I was thinking that I'd probably learned more about the cultural history of England and France than I knew about my own country, and I wanted to put that right. The only place I'd been to in Umbria was Orvieto, which happens to be on the A1 autostrada from Rome. So I spent a really good ten days based in Perugia. There is such a lot to see in this part of the country. But I do remember the wonderful Perugino frescoes in that room."

"What struck me about them was the way they illustrate so vividly what was happening in the Renaissance," he said. "On the ceiling he has the gods of Classical times, with humanist virtues personified on a couple of walls, and on another wall the Hebrew god is enthroned in glory – the two sources of our civilization displayed in comfortable harmony. He wouldn't have got away with that when the Counter-Reformation started imposing 'theological correctness' – like poor old Veronese with his rejected 'Last Supper'."

"So you're interested in Italian art?"

"It gives me an excuse to keep coming back to enjoy your wonderful food," he replied. "Actually my interest was first stimulated by my Uncle

14

Daniel. He and my Aunty Ruth used to come and 'babysit' with me and my sister when we were kids. He'd served in the Army here during the War and the glimpses he'd had of some of the great pictures made him want to come back afterwards to see more. They used to tell us about holidays they'd had, visiting churches and art galleries. They really loved the work of Piero della Francesca, and years later that inspired my first trip to Umbria, at a time, as it happens, when I was trying to get away from unhappy memories."

"Memories connected with the divorce?" she asked, and he nodded in reply.

The waiter came to take their plates and Dan persuaded her to accompany him in sampling the tiramisu, which didn't disappoint. Ordering decaffeinated coffee, he recounted how he had learnt to avoid pronouncing the h in 'Café Hag', and she laughingly affirmed that Italians had no use for aspirates.

All too soon it was time to settle the very reasonable bill and prepare to return to the hotel near the Arco d'Augusto where all the conference members had been lodged. As they stood up at the table she delighted and surprised him by saying, "I don't want this evening to end yet. I have so much enjoyed talking to you."

"Then why don't we go back by a long way round?" he suggested. "There's a bit of the old city that sticks out into the plain like a peninsula, with a big church at the end. I think it's called San Pietro. We could walk out there and look at the lights down below us – and above us."

"I would love to do that. It would certainly be a long way round," she said, with shining eyes that attested to her sincerity. And so, accompanied by the warm good wishes, in Italian and English, of the elderly waiter, they set out on their walk through the narrow, winding streets. In the dim light the medieval appearance of the city was heightened; and at every corner they looked out for the ancient name of the street – Via Baldo, Via Baglioni, Via Oberdan, Via Ercolano. On one steep incline Gina stumbled on the rubble from a pipe-repairers' open trench and he caught her by the arm and waist to steady her.

"This one should be called 'Via Break-a-leg'," she said, smiling her thanks.

When at last they reached the tree-lined Frontone Garden beside the Church of San Pietro they found it deserted, apart from a couple on a bench who were intimately entwined in a passionate embrace. Walking to the farthest boundary wall they looked out at the pinpoints and blotches of light scattered across the plain below.

"That must be Assisi over there," said Gina, pointing to a higher cluster of lights in the far distance.

"I've always had a certain admiration for Saint Francis, in spite of his psychological problems," said Dan. "He at least injected some elements of human kindness into the medieval Church, even though the end result, I suppose, was to shore up its weakening authority for another hundred years or so."

"When I was a little girl I think he was my favourite saint – and we had a lot to choose from. Making friends with Brother Wolf at Gubbio was one of the stories I liked best. Have you been to Gubbio?"

"Yes. It was not very long after the earthquake and they were still doing a lot of rebuilding. It's a beautiful compact old place, perched up there on its hillside. When you stand in that wide piazza looking at the Palazzo dei Consoli you could be right back in the Fourteenth Century." Hesitantly, and trying to sound casual, he added, "When you came to Umbria was it a family holiday or were you on your own?"

"On my own. Bruno was at school – it was term-time; and Guido isn't interested in the past. I think he would go along with Henry Ford's famous dictum."

"Too many people do. In my opinion, if you treat history as 'bunk' you wake up one day to discover it's a bunk you've fallen out of."

Gina laughed with the throaty chuckle he was now beginning to expect. "In English you have a lot of words that sound the same but have completely different meanings. I used to encourage my students to make lists of them."

"You no longer do any teaching?" he asked.

"I stopped when I became pregnant with Bruno. Guido had been reluctant to let me continue after we were married, but at that time we needed the money and so he let me stay in the job."

"Do you have just one child?" he asked.

"Like most Italian families now we have just one child, in spite of what the Pope has been telling us we ought to do. But most of us still go to church on Sunday – well, maybe not every week."

A catch in her voice impelled him to glance sideways at her face, and in the lamplight he saw the glint of a tear trickling down her cheek.

"Oh, I am sorry. Have I said something to upset you?" he exclaimed.

"No, no. I am being stupid. But just before I came here there was a problem with Bruno. I suddenly remembered it."

"If it would help to tell me about it you can, but only if you want to."

"It's really Guido's mother who is the problem," she said, brushing away the tear with the back of her hand. "She has never approved of me, and once I had provided the necessary heir I think she has seen me as an intruder who disturbs the way that the family should be functioning. For years she has tried to turn Bruno against me – like giving him little presents of things that she knew I didn't allow him to have. At first Guido used to laugh and make light of it, and now he has lost interest and doesn't care.

"Last weekend we had a short holiday together, the four of us, in Portofino. Guido was meeting someone there and I think he wanted it to look like an accidental meeting. I had an argument with Bruno about some boys he wanted to keep company with – reckless little snobs, a year or two older than him. But he was rude to me and said terrible things. It has never happened before."

She began to cry, quietly but with shaking shoulders. Tentatively Dan put an arm around her, holding her lightly. "Teenage boys can be unkind without really meaning to be. I'm sure I did it myself. But did your husband know about this?"

"He didn't care," she replied, searching her small, white handbag for a handkerchief. "He hasn't cared much about what happens to me since Bruno was born. This time he just said it was good that Bruno was learning to stand up for himself. I used to think it was his mother poisoning his mind against me, but I found out it was more than that. He had started having other women, and after a while he didn't care that I knew about it. The mistress he has now he has had for six years, and I think she is not the only one. I am just part of his public relations equipment. He wears me on his arm at the Party conference or the *festa dell' amicizia* or the opera. I think he would like to hang me up in the cupboard in between the times when he needs to show me off."

As she wiped her eyes and blew her nose he asked, "If it has been bad for so long why haven't you left him?"

"It is not so easy. I talked to him once about it and he made it plain that he would keep Bruno from me and let his mother look after him. He has a lot of influence, you know, and divorce doesn't fit into his plans. So long as I keep up appearances and don't make a fuss he doesn't mind what I do. I have my own car, and I have time to do what I want to do, and a fair amount of money to spend. I suppose we have had a kind of understanding; and while I have had Bruno I haven't minded so very much, though I have missed having someone… someone to be with. I have missed that very much."

"I am so sorry," said Dan, gently hugging her shoulders. "I hope it has helped a little bit, just talking about it."

"Yes, it has. I don't know why, but when we first met I had a feeling that you were someone I could talk to. It's the first time I've told anyone else about Guido. When the trouble began I talked to my sister, Elena, but she wanted me to go for a divorce and a big alimony payment. After that I didn't talk to her any more. I didn't want my mother to be upset by hearing about it. So I've pretended with the family that everything is all right. While I've had Bruno I've been able to cope, but now I feel that he's starting to move away from me…" She began to cry again.

Dan felt the warmth of her body alongside him, and with the arm encircling her shoulders he drew her a little closer. Instantly she responded, turning towards him so that her left breast was touching his chest, its soft

18

impact sending a shock wave through him. He extended his other arm to encircle her completely, and she buried her face in his neck, sobbing. For several minutes he held her close, and four times he lightly kissed the top of her head, not knowing whether she had felt the contact of his lips through her hair.

"I shouldn't be doing this. It isn't fair to you," she said, raising her head to look up at him. Her eyes were still glistening with tears but they had lost the look of anguish that had been in them a few minutes before.

"Of course you should. It's good for me as much as I hope it is for you. We've both been cast adrift and left to float on our own, and now by chance we've bumped into each other." He drew her gently closer and thrilled to the softness of her breasts as they squeezed against him. "Maybe we can do each other some good – even if it's only a cuddle."

He felt her arms around his waist, holding him tightly. "It's been such a long time since anyone cuddled me," she said. "I miss it almost as much as…" Very lightly she kissed his right cheek.

Dan loosened his embrace of her shoulders so that he could draw back a little and look into her eyes. They were eager and expectant, and as his mouth advanced towards hers she closed them. There could be no mistaking the hunger with which she accepted his kiss.

Again and again they kissed, their bodies pressed ever more closely together. After each kiss he felt as if an invisible wall shutting him off from his own emotions had been broken down; and he wondered whether she was having the same experience. Her arms were round his neck now, and he could feel her fingers caressing the back of his head.

Suddenly she broke away. "It won't do," she said. "We bump into each other but then we have to separate again. Tomorrow evening we have the party for everyone and then on Tuesday we both have to go home. So before we can start to be together we have to be apart again."

Grasping her tightly by her upper arms he exclaimed, "No! We mustn't let that happen. There is so much we can give each other. Why don't you come and meet me in London just as soon as you're able to arrange it? You could call it a shopping expedition. Let me know when you'd like to come and I'll arrange to take some holiday. I haven't had any for a couple of years. We'll do whatever you want to do."

"*Meraviglioso!*" she cried, and once again threw her arms around his neck. But after one more passionate kiss she stepped back, saying, "I want to carry on from there when we meet again in London."

"My arms will be aching to hold you," he said, surprising himself by his choice of words. Their conversation on the way back through the winding streets was, by unspoken mutual consent, devoid of any emotional content.

CHAPTER THREE 5 April, 1989

Dan waited a little apprehensively for his new, temporary, PA to bring in the morning mail. He had met her only once before, when he interviewed her for the post with the help of Anne, his very pregnant PA. They had both liked the young Canadian and, in spite of her lack of office experience, had been confident that she would be able to keep things running smoothly for the next six months. But now that the change was actually happening he was conscious of just how much he had relied on being supported by someone who, over the five years she had been in the job, had become able almost to read his thoughts and anticipate his requests.

"Good morning, Mary," he said as she entered carrying the green in-tray, full of paper.

"Good morning, Mr Leyland," she responded. "I hope everything went well in Italy."

"Please call me Dan," he said. "Everyone else does. And I hope you won't mind if I don't address you as Miss Burns."

She laughed and said, "I think we're still a bit more formal in Canada, at least in some places. I had a temporary job in a law firm in Halifax after I graduated, and they were a bit starchy."

"The conference in Italy went well, thanks," he said, beginning to glance through the pile of papers in the tray.

"I've tried to put the ones I thought were most urgent on the top," she said, "but of course I don't really know yet what your priorities are. I have made a start, though. Anne spent the day with me on Monday, and that was a tremendous help. But I know it's not going to be easy to fill her place."

"How was she? There's only about a month to go now before the baby arrives."

"She seemed to be very well, but she said she was going to be very bored sitting at home with nothing to do. She was planning to give the house a Spring clean but her husband has insisted that she mustn't do that."

"Anne is always happiest when she's busy - which has been greatly to my advantage," said Dan. "I think you'll find she's left everything in good order for you. The first big task, as she's probably told you, will be the judging of the International Development Enterprise Awards. We've already completed the first stage and our panels of assessors have selected the short lists. Now we have to get those out to the judges, who'll be meeting in about a fortnight. They're an interesting lot. I think you'll enjoy meeting them."

"The letter on top is from one of them - Sir Peter somebody, I think - who says he can't manage the date now because he's unexpectedly been told he must attend a consultation in Lagos," said Mary. "I suppose that's going to make things difficult for you."

"It certainly is," he replied, plucking the letter out of the tray and glancing at it. "We can't alter the date now because six other people are already committed to it; so we're going to have to find a replacement for Sir Peter at short notice. The problem is trying to keep a balance between their different backgrounds. Sir Peter has a Commonwealth connection."

"Would one of the High Commissioners in London be a possibility?" Mary asked.

"If there was more time that could be worth thinking about, but diplomats are usually booked up well in advance. However, you've given me an idea. There's a retired Indian Army general who spends about half the year in London, pursuing business interests. I think he's here at the moment. Sensible chap and good company. I'll give him a ring this morning."

"Shall I start preparing a mailing to the judges?"

"Please do. I'm sure Anne has left you a draft, but if there's anything you don't understand just ask me. You'll see that we have some interesting contenders this year. There's one in the 'Long-term Commitment' category that's very typical of what we're trying to publicise and encourage. Read through that write-up and it'll give you a good idea of what the Awards are all about. It's a Midlands engineering company that's been building up a network of partnerships with companies in developing countries for nearly forty years. It licenses them to manufacture components for engines used in tractors and trucks, and backs that up with training and help with factory lay-out and quality control. Over the years it must have helped to create hundreds of jobs in about a dozen countries. And, of course, the profits earned and the taxes paid have all helped to build up their economies."

"Yes, I'll certainly read that," said Mary, "and the other write-ups too, because I'd like to know what it's all about."

As he went through the rest of the letters in the tray Dan found little else of particular interest. "This enquiry from the Business Studies teacher should go to John Hogan, our Academic Liaison Officer," he said. "I expect Anne introduced you to him."

"Yes, she did. I feel I know everybody quite well already - but with only five of us that's not difficult."

"As time goes by you'll find there are a number of other people who do particular jobs for us on a freelance basis," he said. "Some of them have very interesting backgrounds - like David, who'll be working on the brochure about the Awards. I'm sure you'll very quickly get to know them. I don't think I have any appointments in the diary today. Have you checked?"

"Oh, yes. Anne gave me strict instructions that was the first thing I must do every morning, and last thing at the end of the day, to check on tomorrow's engagements."

Dan smiled. "Yes, she doesn't trust my memory, and very wisely too, because I sometimes get preoccupied with what I happen to be doing.

"Since there's nothing in the diary I may leave a little bit early this afternoon, because I need to check on the arrangements for a family event that's going to take place tomorrow evening. It's my parents' fiftieth wedding anniversary and I've arranged a celebration dinner with a few friends and family. Needless to say, Anne helped me a lot with getting things together."

"Fifty years? Does that mean they got married when the War began?" Mary asked.

"Actually it was about six months before. The timing was determined by the fact that my mother was a refugee from the Spanish Civil War and our government had just recognized the Franco regime. So they were worried by a rumour that refugees might be sent back to Spain. Because they were in a hurry they actually got married at Gretna Green. Have you heard of that place in Scotland, where the blacksmith used to marry people - usually runaway couples who didn't have parental consent?"

"Yes, I have, actually. My grandfather was a migrant from Scotland and there was always a lot of talk in the family about old Scottish customs"

"Was he by any chance related to Scotland's great poet?"

"I don't think so, for I'm sure we would have heard all about it if he had been. But he did actually come from Ayrshire. I'd like to go there sometime while I'm over here."

"Are you still in touch with relatives in Scotland?"

"The contacts faded out after Grandpa died. He was the youngest in his family and his siblings had all died some years earlier. Do you still have contacts with relations in Spain?"

"No. There were no close relatives still alive after the War; and my mother was very determined that she was going to be British. The only reminder is my middle name."

"The C? I've seen that on a document. What does it stand for?"

"Carlos. It was my grandfather's name. And I did learn Spanish, which has been useful in work - though not in this particular job. Anyhow, I'm sure there'll be a lot of nostalgia around tomorrow evening."

"Will it involve people travelling through the West End?" she asked, with a slightly anxious expression. "I read in the paper that Mr Gorbachev is going to have dinner at Downing Street tomorrow evening, and I suppose there might be some disruption of the traffic."

"That's a good point," he replied, "but I don't think it's likely to have a serious effect on the traffic - though we are dining not far away from there, at the Travellers' Club in Pall Mall. I've been a member there for a long time."

"Will this be Mr Gorbachev's first visit to London?" she asked.

"No. He came here a few years ago, actually before he became boss of the USSR. I think that was when Mrs Thatcher decided he was someone she 'could do business with'."

"It would sure be great if she can encourage him to go on with making things easier for people in East Europe," said Mary. "It was really amazing hearing about the elections in Russia last week."

"Yes. I expect he'll need all the encouragement he can get now. I would guess it's going to be a tricky time for him and Yeltsin. The die-hard Communists must be thinking that their last chance of hanging on to power is starting to slip away from them, and they're not going to give up easily."

"I'd love to visit Leningrad while I'm over here," she said, "and see all those wonderful paintings in the Hermitage."

"That would be a good trip to make, if you can afford it. There are some really remarkable things to see. And with any luck the food might have improved since I was there, about a year ago. But try to avoid going in the winter. That was a mistake I made."

"We're well used to hard winters in Canada," she said, smiling, "though actually Halifax isn't too bad - not like Ottawa or Winnipeg."

Dan glanced at his watch. "We'd better get down to work now. I have a lot to catch up with. Could you bring me in the Awards Judges file, please? I'll see if I can get the General on the phone."

"Do you happen to know if that's filed under D for 'Development' or A for 'Awards'?" she enquired.

"If I remember correctly it's under A."

"I'll fetch it right away," she said, and as she closed the door behind her Dan felt reassured that he was not going to be deprived of the support system on which he had been so relaxedly relying.

CHAPTER FOUR 6 April, 1989

The celebratory meal had gone well. As the waiter arrived with the coffee Dan looked around the oval table and reflected how comfortably it accommodated a group of twelve. It might have been a tight squeeze if Nancy's son, Leo, and his wife, Emma, had been able to accept their invitation.

"Nancy, I'm sorry Leo and Emma weren't able to be with us. He's the only absentee from those times long ago when we all used to get together," he said.

"He was sorry, too," Nancy replied, "but you know how conscientious he is. He's the chairman of this little House of Lords group that has gone to Zambia and he felt that he had to be with them."

"He has done some really useful work in the years since he took his seat in the Lords," said Ruth. "I remember having a long chat with him when he was trying to decide whether or not to take up the peerage, and he wasn't at all confident that he had the ability to put it to good use politically. Time has certainly proved that he had."

"I was talking to a lobby correspondent a few months ago who said he thought your son was one of the most effective of the Crossbenchers in the Lords. It was after he'd asked that question about monitoring the crisis in Kosovo," said Arthur.

Dan nodded his head in approval of his father's comment; and Nancy replied, "I remember him asking me whether I thought his father would have approved of him taking his seat. That was a difficult question to answer because, of course, Freddie had never expected to succeed to the title, being the younger son. When he did succeed, because of his father's unexpected death, it was only a few weeks before he was killed. But in the last letter he wrote to me from Greece - it arrived only after I'd heard about his death - he said he might take his seat in the Lords after the War because it would give him a platform to campaign for the abolition of the place. So I was able to show that to Leo, and I think it helped him to decide. He's in favour of having an elected second chamber, but nothing's going to happen about that until we have a change of government."

"Arthur, do you think there will be a change next time, whenever that may be?" asked Rod (Dan still thought of him as 'Uncle Roddy').

"Very hard to say," Arthur replied. "I think a lot will depend on whether Mrs Thatcher decides to run again. At the moment I don't see Mr Kinnock as a contender the voters would want to have in her place, though he has made a start on trying to talk some sense into his party. As you know, I used to have high hopes for the Social Democrats, but after last year's merger with the Liberals I don't think there's much hope for a strong party in the centre ground of politics. Our 'first past the post' system makes most people think they can only choose the lesser of two evils."

"So you think we might actually have a fourth Thatcher government?" asked Rebecca.

"Well, as I said, it might depend on whether the lady decides to run again herself. But even if she doesn't Labour will need to have made some big changes before the election if people are going to trust it to manage the economy," Arthur replied.

"When you were an MP was there the same kind of bickering inside the Labour Party?" asked his grandson, George.

"There were plenty of dissenting voices and some of them were inside the government. But all major political parties have to be coalitions of different interest groups under our electoral system. If they weren't they wouldn't attract enough support to win an election. The alternative is to have some kind of proportional representation, where every interest group has its own political party and several of them have to get together in a coalition to form a government. Back in '45 I sat on the Government benches with a broad range of people, from closet communists who knew they'd never get elected if they admitted their objectives, to liberal-minded social reformers who had to pretend to be socialists. The amazing thing was that Clem Attlee managed to keep them all together to run the country for six years."

"Maybe what Labour needs now is another Attlee," Rod observed.

"There's a particular problem when a party is in Opposition," said Arthur. "The MPs who have been elected come mainly from the safe seats - by definition - and a high proportion of them tend to be more ideologically extreme. The same thing applies to the Tories as well as to Labour. And because the voices of MPs are the ones that predominate, the party can get increasingly out of touch with the way that people are thinking across the country. It can create a kind of vicious circle of introspection that keeps the party out of power. Attlee had a lot more problems in the pre-War period than he did in government, I think. The Labour Party now is going to need some clever leadership if it's going to get re-elected to power."

"Did you have much contact with Mr Attlee when you were in Parliament, Grandpa?" asked Brenda.

"Not much personal contact though, of course, I saw quite a lot of him in meetings of the Parliamentary Party and so on. My last contact with him was amusing - in a sad sort of way. It must have been about a dozen years after he'd ceased to be PM. I was invited to a dinner - at the House, as it happened - given by a charity I'd been helping at the time. They'd also invited Clem, who by that time was an earl, of course. Presumably they wanted to add gravitas to the occasion. Anyhow, he'd been asked to propose the Loyal Toast and he got to his feet, a little bit shakily, and said, 'Ladies and gentlemen, the King!' I noticed that those who gave a verbal response were trying to make 'The Queen' sound like 'The King' to spare him embarrassment. But that was the last time I saw him."

"Which reminds me that we have not yet had a toast to the bride and groom," said Daniel. (Dan still instinctively thought of him as 'Uncle Daniel' even though he had long since ceased to use the title.) So they all raised their glasses to "Margarita and Arthur".

"We don't need any speeches this evening," said Arthur, "but we do want to say thank you to all of you for being here, and for the friendships that have lasted for so many decades. I remember all the happy occasions when those of you who are now septuagenarians got together with us in days long gone, around tables in all kinds of different places, in the years both before and after the War. The menus were sometimes a lot more limited than today, but the conversation and the good companionship were always the same. I hope they'll last for another decade, at least."

28

"And it pleases us a lot to see two more generations joining in tonight," Margarita added. "I hope that all your friendships will be as long-lasting."

"You've set us a good example," said her grandson, George.

His sister, Brenda, added, "I've already lost touch with most of the girls I was at school with, apart from one. I suppose we're at the stage where you're able to start picking out the people who are on the same wavelength as yourself - the ones you're likely to have a long-term relationship with."

"You've had two terms at LSE now. Have you found it easy to get to know people?" Daniel asked her. "It's a much bigger place now than it was when your grandfather and I were postgraduates there."

"I've been lucky enough to get a place in Passfield Hall," she replied. "It's much easier getting to know people when you live in the same hall of residence. Had it opened when you were at LSE?"

"I don't remember it; but in those days it would certainly have been a 'men only' establishment."

"Like the 'girls only' establishment where Ruth and I first met," said Nancy. "We're still in touch with a few of the others from those pre-War days, though we haven't organized any kind of reunion for quite some time now. When was the last one, Ruth?"

"It must have been about four or five years ago. I remember Mr Gorbachev had just been on his first visit here, but he hadn't yet become leader of the Soviet Union. That's stuck in my memory because Dodie was very dismissive about him. She said he was only pretending to be nice in order to lull Mrs Thatcher into a sense of false security, and in the end he'd turn out to be like all the rest of them. Luckily it seems that she was wrong."

"She was; and I hope we're going to grab hold of the opportunity that seems to be opening up while he's in charge," said Daniel. "I don't know what Mrs Thatcher will be saying to him today, but it ought to go a lot farther than Anglo-Soviet relations. When I was working at the UN in 1946 - albeit in a very lowly capacity - a lot of people hoped we could make the organization into an effective instrument for preventing aggression. It was a lost cause, of course, because Stalin was hell-bent on being an aggressor himself and he had a veto on the Security Council. But this man, Gorbachev, genuinely seems to want Russia to be part of the international community. So now is the time to start thinking again about giving the UN a peace-keeping rôle that amounts to more than stepping in to save face when the combatants have reached a stalemate."

"Are you thinking in terms of a permanent UN rapid intervention force? I remember that was talked about back in the '40s," Arthur asked.

"Yes, something of that kind. But it would only work if the trigger for action was virtually automatic. A would-be aggressor would need to be quite sure that if he invaded his neighbour the intervention force would be on his doorstep next morning - followed up, of course, by whatever international back-up might be needed. But if enough time was left for a *fait accompli* by the aggressor while a UN committee was being convened, and while sympathetic would-be aggressors in other countries pleaded his case, the aggressor might not be deterred. As Jim Callaghan once said, 'A lie can be half-way around the world before the truth has got its boots on.'"

"Do you think it should be a kind of multinational force, with mixed personnel, rather than one made up of units seconded from different countries?" asked Rod.

"I do, even though I know there would be problems about language; but those problems would always exist anyhow, only at a different level of command. You must have seen it working yourself, when you were in the International Brigade."

"Yes, I did; and we managed pretty well," Rod replied. "And the other side had their Foreign Legion, who were also a pretty lethal bunch."

Daniel nodded in assent and continued, "One advantage of having multinational personnel would be to cut out the inevitable lobbying by isolationists saying, 'Don't send our boys to fight in a war that doesn't appear to threaten our own security.' I can still remember reading the correspondence columns in the newspapers when I was on my way to Korea. And of course if the pause is long enough they'll be joined… joined by…"

Dan noticed the sudden hesitation in Daniel's voice and guessed the reason for it. He had probably been about to say something like 'joined by the usual suspects waving banners proclaiming *Give Peace a Chance'*, and had then remembered Nancy's presence and wanted to avoid giving her offence.

Sure enough, Daniel continued, "joined by politicians with axes to grind. One way or another, the bully boys would have long enough to grab what they wanted and hope for a stalemate. But I doubt if anyone is seriously thinking about this moment as a second chance to create a really new international order - and that's what we're going to need in the next century."

"Isn't it really the veto that's at the root of the problem?" Arthur asked. "The only time there's ever been a full-blown UN intervention to resist an aggressor was in Korea, when the Russians happened to be boycotting the Security Council and a resolution was able to be passed without the veto being used."

"Exactly so," said Daniel. "And if the Russians had been there and used the veto then every idealistic internationalist and every fellow-traveller, from Camden Town to California, would have screamed, 'Illegal! Breach of the UN Charter! American imperialism!' if we'd taken action to protect the South Koreans. There has got to be a different system, where international law is not designed to protect the lawbreakers rather than their victims; and now we might have the best opportunity we'll have for a long time to get some general agreement on making a fresh start."

"Don't you think the priority ought to be disarmament?" asked Nancy.

"I think it should," Daniel replied, "but that's only going to happen on a worldwide scale if countries can be confident that the international community is not only willing but also able to come to their aid if they're attacked by a neighbour. Reagan and Gorbachev have already made a promising start on the nuclear weapons sector, but getting down to the level of howitzers and Kalashnikovs is going to need something a lot more reassuring for the people who own them - and there are far too many of them, all round the world. If every country could be persuaded to put, say ten percent, of its current defence budget into the creation of an international peacekeeping force, then it might have the confidence to cut the remainder of its arms expenditure by fifty per cent."

"Do you think there's a real chance that something of that kind could actually happen?" asked George; and Dan noted the expression of genuine interest on his youthful face.

"I wish I did," Daniel replied. "Back in 1945 a lot of people were hopeful that we could create a new international system for keeping the peace."

"Just as in 1919 a lot of people thought they'd finished fighting the war to end all wars," said Arthur.

"But at least we've learned a lot of lessons from their mistakes," said Ruth. "We've kept the peace between the big powers for twice the length of time that they managed; and if the Cold War is really coming to an end now it could be realistic to start thinking about new ways of bringing peace to other parts of the world. It's a job for your generation to do, Bob and Vera and Dan. It could be too late by the time Brenda and George's generation are in control."

"Don't look at me," said Vera smiling. "I'm not into politics. Actually, I used to be a member of UNA, but it seems to have fizzled out in our part of the world."

"When is your next book coming out, Ruth?" Rebecca asked. "Isn't it going to be about somebody working at the League of Nations in the 1920s?"

"Yes. I had a lot of fun finding out about life in Geneva in those optimistic years. And, of course, my character takes holiday breaks in Grindelwald, just as I used to do myself, only about ten years later."

"It's a sobering thought that younger readers are going to see your book as an 'historical novel', even though it's set in a time from which people of our generation still have vivid childhood memories," said Rebecca. "I can remember standing in the Schönbrunn Palace gardens, holding my mother's hand and listening to a brass band more clearly than I can remember last week's concert at the Wigmore Hall."

"I suppose it was Strauss the band was playing," said Arthur.

"It was, and I was enjoying it; but nowadays when I hear a piece by Strauss I feel slightly nauseated. Those hearty tunes remind me inevitably of that hypocritical generation who packed the streets to welcome Hitler and who nowadays whinge about having been invaded and having no option but to obey the Nazis."

Dan remembered that her family had all perished in the Holocaust and he understood the emotion in her voice.

"Memories can often be bittersweet," said his mother. "My first year at university in Salamanca was happy and exciting, but I can't think of it now without remembering the dreadful things that happened in the year I graduated - and afterwards."

"We're very lucky never to have had that kind of experience," said his brother-in-law, Bob. "I can remember being old enough to feel worried when I heard the grown-ups talking about the war in Korea, but National Service had ended by the time I was old enough to have been called up. Ruth's right when she says it's the job of our generation to grab this opportunity. We have to try again for a better way of keeping the peace, but I haven't heard any of the politicians talking about it. And I suppose that's because not many of the voters are interested in international affairs."

"It was always like that," said Arthur. "I remember trying to talk about international issues like the UN at meetings during the '45 election but my agent, dear old Bill Coverdale - do you remember him? - told me it was a waste of time. What people wanted to know about was how quickly we could put the Beveridge Plan into action and get a health service and improve the schools. They'd had enough of trying to put the world to rights."

"As it happens, there really was no way we could have done that in '45, but there might just be an opportunity now," said Daniel. "Unfortunately the message that the politicians get from the media and the voters, is that winning the gratitude of their grandchildren by creating a more stable world isn't something that'll get them back into the next parliament."

"Being just an engineer, I feel there's not much I can do about it," said Bob.

"H G Wells once suggested that the way to have a peaceful world would be to put the engineers in charge of it," said Ruth. "He might have had a point."

"Didn't Wells get himself an interview with Stalin some time in the '30s?" asked Rod.

"Yes, and I don't think Stalin knew what to make of him," said Ruth. "At that time a lot of our leading intellectuals seem to have been pretty naïve."

"They weren't the only ones," said Daniel. "And we had to pay the price for our wishful thinking later on. It's ironic that it should have been left to first Khrushchev and now Gorbachev to finally explode the myths about the benevolence of Marx-Leninism. I wonder what will be the next ism to lead us down a primrose path to destruction."

"There would appear to be some among the environmentalists who would like to lead us off in that direction," said Arthur. "Every ism has some plausible arguments in its favour before it falls into the hands of the megalomaniacs."

"Speaking of megalomaniacs, we're going to see *Henry VI* at the Barbican tomorrow," said Rod. "I've heard it's a good production. It's the first part of a Shakespeare trilogy the RSC has put together. They're calling it *The Plantaganets*."

"We're seeing the second and third parts on Saturday afternoon and evening," Rebecca added. "It's going to be quite a marathon."

"Is your dramatic society working on anything at the moment?" Margarita asked.

"Yes. We're putting on *Arms and the Man* at the end of the month. For some reason it has been difficult finding rehearsal dates that suited everybody this time, even though it's not a huge cast; but there are a couple of young marrieds with children among the cast, and weekends can be difficult for them," Rod replied.

"We'd like to have tickets for that," said Daniel. "Shaw is always entertaining. Do you remember when we trod the boards together at Trinity in *The Devil's Disciple*?"

"I do, indeed," said Rod. "Daniel played General Burgoyne to my Dick Dudgeon. I don't think either of us thought then we'd ever be engaged in actual warfare, and yet it was only a few years before we were."

"And even if Daniel didn't become a general he made it all the way to colonel, which wasn't bad after starting as a private," Dan observed.

"We all soon found ourselves in situations we would never have dreamed of," said Ruth. "That's what happens when people you thought had nothing to do with you suddenly become the reason why your life has to change."

"And if, like you were saying earlier, the politicians of my generation make the right decisions now, then the future should be a lot more predictable for George and Brenda's generation," said Dan.

"I'm not sure that I want things to be predictable," said George. "A bit of uncertainty can make life more exciting."

"But not the kind of uncertainty that comes in the shape of bombs and bullets," said Nancy.

CHAPTER FIVE 12-13 June, 1989

As Mary came into his office carrying the post Dan remarked, "I saw you at the concert yesterday afternoon but you were too far away for me to catch your eye. I didn't know you were interested in classical music."

"It's been one of those things that's been really good for me in London. There are so many opportunities to hear great music," she replied. "And yesterday was the first time I've ever seen a woman conducting. Jane Glover was terrific, wasn't she? I think the Thirty-fifth is my favourite Mozart symphony."

"It's one of my favourites, too," he said, impressed by her enthusiasm. "You've probably noticed that concerts here are less expensive than the theatre nowadays. London theatre prices seem to be really spiralling. I think they're fuelled by the tourist trade."

"What did the panel of judges decide on Friday?" Mary asked, sitting down in front of his desk.

"They finally decided on the Kenya sugar project for the Sustainable Development Award. They were particularly impressed by the way that the company has made use of so many thousands of 'outgrowers' instead of relying on a plantation to supply the factory. And the fact that Kenyans have been trained to head all five departments was another strong point."

"Did anyone mention the football team?" she asked.

"Yes, the General was very keen on that - though I know he's a cricket fan himself. But he waxed quite lyrical about the value of sport in creating a new community. It'll all be in the brochure. The Long-term Commitment Award went to the engine-building company. I thought at one point the tractor-repair project was going to be the favourite, but they decided that the engines had a longer track record, and they were impressed by how much know-how had been transferred. Anyhow, our next challenge is going to be persuading people to come to the awards ceremony. I'll be drafting some more invitation letters later on today. "Anything interesting in the post?"

"It's mostly the usual Monday morning stuff, but there's a letter from Botswana that might be connected to the chat you had with the High Commissioner in May."

"I hope it is. If one of their ministers is willing to do a Development Leadership Visit for us it could have a lot of different angles. Let's open that one straight away."

Mary handed him the envelope, already slit open. He extracted the letter and quickly glanced through it. "Brilliant!" he exclaimed. "The Commerce minister would like to come, and he might be able to bring Lady Khama along with him."

"Who is Lady Khama?"

"Nowadays she is known in Botswana as 'Mother of the Chief'. Her late husband, Seretse Khama, was the first president of the country, and there was a tremendous international fuss about forty years ago when he decided to marry her. He was student in London at the time and she was a London-born girl who was working as a clerk. But his father was Chief of the biggest tribe in what was then Bechuanaland, and in those days the idea of a black man marrying a white woman was very disturbing to a lot of people. However, Ruth and Seretse stuck to their guns and the story eventually had a happy ending. I think he died about ten years ago, but she has remained an influential figure in the country."

"She must be a very interesting person. I hope she'll come."

"I'll do a reply to the letter later on today," said Dan. "In the meantime I'll have a quick glance through the rest of the post and then I'll give you some more invitation letters for the Awards ceremony."

* * *

Dan had just completed a personalized invitation to an old acquaintance at the BBC World Service when his telephone rang. "There's a call from Italy for you," said Mary when he answered. "Her name sounded like Gina Urbisaggia."

"Oh, that's the Contessa. Put her through, please."

A slight echo distorted Gina's voice, but he could still detect the warm musicality that had given him so much pleasure. "Dan, I am sorry to telephone you at your office, but I wanted to ask you something as quickly as I could," she said.

"I don't mind where or when you ring, Gina. Your calls will always be welcome. What's the news?"

"Guido has announced that he's going to Hong Kong on business at the beginning of July. I thought it might be a good time to have my shopping trip to London, but only if you are going to be around at that time."

"Brilliant!" he exclaimed, experiencing an unfamiliar sensation of hope. "The first week in July is going to be a lull period for me, before a busy few days leading up to the business awards ceremony - I think I told you about them."

"Yes, you did. That's all I needed to know. I'll try to make a booking today, and I'll telephone you this evening with the details. Will you be at home?"

"I'll be sitting by the telephone," he replied.

* * *

When Mary came into his office with the post next morning he told her he would be taking the first week of July as holiday.

"Going anywhere exciting?" she asked.

"Yes and no. There are things I want to be doing in London, and I hope that some of them will turn out to be quite exciting. It should be a quiet time here, and if you want to take a day or two off in the middle of the week, feel free. You have my home number if there should be any emergency; but you'd need to ring either very early or very late in the day, because I expect I'll be out a lot. Or, of course, you can always leave a message."

"I'm pretty sure I won't need to trouble you," said Mary, smiling. "I was thinking I might go to Oxford for a day. I guess there'd be lots to see in that city."

"There certainly would be. Apart from the famous old colleges and churches, there's a very good art gallery and museum called the Ashmolean. Are you interested in art?"

"It's one of the main reasons I'm over here. We don't have a lot in Canada - at least not much of the old stuff."

"You'll find plenty of that in the Ashmolean. The picture galleries are a manageable size for a short visit, and they have a really representative range of artists, all the way from Bellini and Giorgione to Van Gogh and Picasso."

"Is there anything in particular I should look out for?"

"I was particularly intrigued by their Uccello. It's called 'Hunt in the Forest' and it shows a throng of huntsmen, some mounted and some on foot, with their hounds, moving through a dark forest of trees that have had their lower branches lopped off so that the mounted men don't bang their heads. And it's all done with Uccello's obsessive attention to perspective."

"Wasn't he the artist whose wife is supposed to have called him to bed when he was sitting up at night working out calculations for the vanishing-point?"

"He's the one," Dan replied, impressed by her evident interest in the history of art. "It's a strange picture and no one knows much about its origin, though it's assumed that one of the Medici must have commissioned it. They also have a strange Bronzino portrait of a much later Medici, one of the sons of Cosimo I, as a precocious and slightly sinister-looking young boy. I read somewhere - in the caption, I suppose - that he was made a cardinal when he was sixteen; but he didn't live very long. Anyhow, I think you'll find plenty to interest you."

"I'll definitely go on one of the days when you're on holiday," she said. "There doesn't seem to be much excitement about the build-up to the European Election on Thursday. I mentioned it to a couple of people who didn't even know it was happening."

"I think a lot of people are not convinced that voting would make any difference to what actually happens in Brussels," he replied, "and in a sense they are right. Most ordinary people seem to have an instinctive feel for where power is really located, even when they haven't bothered to think about it, and they know that it's not in the European Parliament. It never will be unless there is a real European federation, like the USA - or Canada - and if that happens I don't think Britain will be a member of it. But I'm not sure that many of the voters, as distinct from the politicians, in the other countries want it to happen, either."

"I'm really looking forward to starting my trip to Europe in the autumn - not that I won't be sorry to be leaving the job. I'm really enjoying working here," she added hastily.

"I'm glad you are, but a trip through Europe will be an exciting adventure for you. Before you leave we must have a chat about the places you're going to visit. I might be able to give you a few tips about some of them.

"Now, what's in the tray today? Are there any acceptances from journalists for the meeting with the World Bank chap on the capital needs of developing countries?"

"I think there are three or four. I noticed the *Economist* and the *Financial Times.*"

"That sounds promising. He's a good speaker - we've had him before. I hope we won't have lots of empty seats, like we had at the meeting on the UNCTAD annual report."

"I suppose a lot depends on what else is happening on that particular day," she observed. "I've thought about the possibility of trying for a job in journalism when I go home next year. I know it's a risky profession but I think it could be very satisfying. There must be so much variety in what you're doing."

"Maybe we ought to track down some of the Canadian media correspondents in London and send them invitations. Then you might have a chance to chat up one or two of them and find out what the possibilities are back home. It's never too soon to start doing a bit of research. Remind me to have a word later with Derek Ingram at the Commonwealth Journalists' Association. He will probably know who might be interested in having an invitation."

"Thank you very much," said Mary. "That sounds like a great idea. By the way, did you hear that interview on the radio about what's been happening in Poland? It reminded me of what you were saying yesterday about the contrast with the way things have turned out in China, after that awful massacre in Beijing."

"Yes, not long ago the commentators were all predicting that Communism would crumble first in China, the way things were going over there; but now it's in Europe that the dictatorships seem to be falling apart. I think it was Harold Wilson who said that a week is a long time in politics. But you would be too young to remember that."

CHAPTER SIX 30 July, 1989

Gina might be interested in the Italian Hospital, Dan thought as he turned out of Great Ormond Street into Queen Square and the building caught his eye. But he didn't know very much about it, apart from the fact that it had been founded in the late nineteenth century to care for Italian immigrants; and just recently he had read that the building was now being taken over by Great Ormond Street Hospital for Sick Children. She might also be interested to see a traditional English pub, he reflected as, turning into narrow Cosmo Place, he passed 'The Queen's Larder' on the corner.

On the previous evening he hadn't lingered with Gina after escorting her to the Bonnington Hotel. She had looked and sounded weary - though pleased to see him - after her flight from Rome, and he had decided it was not the time for serious conversation, let alone any physical contact beyond the hugs and kisses of arrival, greeting and his good night departure. Now he was uncertain about how best to revive the intimacy they had achieved in Perugia. In the taxi she had said how wonderful it was to be with him again, but her evident tiredness had restrained him from treating her as a lover.

When he entered the hotel lobby she was waiting for him, looking immaculate in a light grey linen suit with white braiding, her feet in 'sensible' low-heeled grey shoes. "Where are you going to take me first?" she asked, between pressing her soft lips to both his cheeks.

"You've said that the National Gallery is high on your wish list. Would you like to start there?"

Within minutes they were seated on a bus heading down Kingsway en route for Trafalgar Square.

* * *

Because he was not well represented in Italian galleries Gina had said she was particularly interested in looking at paintings by Rubens. As they approached his huge 'Peace and War' canvas Dan said, "I think this picture is one that represents Rubens very effectively, the man as well as the artist. There's a tendency in art history circles nowadays to disparage him - 'all buxom women and obscure mythology.' I think that's just contemporary

42

prejudices in the mouths of people who haven't taken the trouble to really look at his pictures."

"This does look a little bit like obscure mythology," said Gina as they halted in front of a crowded array of antique gods, semi-naked women, serious-faced children and a kittenish leopard.

"When it was painted - here in London - the symbolism was bang up-to-date," said Dan. "Rubens was here as an ambassador from the Spanish monarchy, with the job of arranging a peace treaty with Britain, and he succeeded. The voluptuous woman in the centre is Peace, and you can see that she's squirting milk from her breast to the mouth of the infant Plutus, who is the god of wealth. Behind her the woman in black armour is Minerva, the goddess of wisdom, who is protecting Peace from the approach of Mars, the god or war. And the satyr in the foreground is presenting her with a horn of plenty filled with the fruits of the earth. The role of the three children on the right is a bit more obscure, but it's been said that they derive from a Greek poem about Peace as 'Protector of Children'. Apparently they are portraits of the children of the man with whom Rubens was staying in London, a painter called Balthasar Gerbier."

"So it was as up-to-date in its time as Picasso's 'Guernica'," said Gina. "And that made use of mythology, too."

"There's something over there, behind you, that shows just how versatile he was as a painter," said Dan, leading her to another huge canvas, which depicted a vast stretch of open countryside under a wide sky. In the left foreground a farm wagon drawn by two horses was conveying a peasant and his wife, and nearby a hunter with a gun was crouching low to stalk some partridges.

"The grand house on the left, behind the trees, is Rubens' retirement home," he continued. "When he was in his mid-fifties and a widower he married a girl of sixteen, gave up his official duties and settled down there to enjoy life - including painting pictures just for his own pleasure."

"It's a wonderfully tranquil scene," said Gina. "Who are the three tiny figures near to the house?"

"Apparently that is Rubens and his wife out for a morning stroll, with a wet nurse who is suckling their baby."

Gina looked closely at the picture. "So he had a child with his second wife," she said.

"I think he had several. He was also a very good portrait painter, as you can see from this picture over here." Dan moved to one side to stand in front of a half-length portrait of a young woman wearing a wide-brimmed hat. "She is believed to be the older sister of his second wife, though the picture was painted some years before his marriage. He already had connections with her family."

"I like the way he has shown those little wisps of hair sticking out from under her hat, and the way that she isn't looking directly at us, though she does have a friendly face. I think he must have enjoyed painting her," said Gina.

"An interesting fact about this picture is that it directly inspired another artist about a hundred and fifty years later," said Dan, nodding his head in agreement. "And you can see her picture when we go through to the French gallery. It's a self-portrait by Elizabeth Vigée Le Brun, and she actually says in her *Memoirs* that she was trying to achieve the same effect that Rubens did in this painting."

"Oh, I know a little about her," said Gina. "I discovered her paintings when I went to the Louvre a few years ago. There was a beautiful one showing her with her little daughter. Didn't she escape from the French Revolution and go to Italy for a while?"

"Yes, that's the lady. She had a fascinating life, and I think she was a very good artist. We'll be meeting her soon, in her hat, when we go through to the other gallery."

When they had completed their tour of the National Gallery Dan took Gina back to Bloomsbury for lunch at a small Italian restaurant in Theobalds Road where he was a frequent diner, preferring its bustling ambience to the solitary quietness of his flat. Over mushroom risotto and tiramisu they talked about the pictures they had seen that morning, and about the weariness that inevitably accompanied a visit to the endless galleries of the Vatican museum, where she had recently taken her son.

As their *espresso* arrived she asked, "Do you remember that statue they have of a nude man – it's a Roman copy of a Greek original, I think – who is standing with his weight on one leg? It's call the *Doryphoros*. When I looked at it I found myself thinking about you."

Dan laughed. "I'm immensely flattered, but I'm sure I don't deserve the comparison."

Sensing a moment of opportunity, he asked, "Would you really like to make the comparison, even though it's bound to be disappointing? My flat's only a few minutes' walk from here – that's if you'd like a change from more cultural sightseeing."

He detected a slight blush as she replied, "I think that's a great idea. After all, I didn't come to London just for the pictures."

Dan lost no time in paying the bill, and when they had crossed the busy road he led her into Lamb's Conduit Street. Noticing the street sign, she asked him, "Who was Lamb?"

"He was a wealthy clothmaker at the time of the first Queen Elizabeth who connected up some springs of fresh water just north of here to a lead pipe, and ran the pipe along a conduit that took it to the City of London. There it was welcomed by a dense population in need of more water. He was a real entrepreneur."

"The kind that you might have given an award to?" she asked, smiling.

"Exactly so. This is a part of London where a lot of interesting people have lived in times gone by, when it was comparatively inexpensive – writers like Dorothy L Sayers and Wilfred Owen and Ted Hughes, the present Poet Laureate, and his first wife, Sylvia Plath."

"And now you live here."

"Yes, I live in the house with the blue door that we're just coming to," he replied, feeling in his pocket for the key.

Once up the narrow stairs and through the front door of his own flat he was seized by a moment of uncertainty. Had Gina really meant that she wanted to make love? It was so long since he had last had a positive reaction from a woman that he wondered if he was allowing the overwhelming desire, that was even now beginning to manifest itself physically, to get the better of his reason. Could such a beautiful, intelligent and altogether desirable woman – albeit unhappily married – really want to make love with him?"

The front door, which led directly into the living-room, had barely closed behind them when Gina threw her arms around his neck and kissed him passionately on his lips. "I've dreamt so many times of this moment," she said before their lips came together again.

"So have I," he said, "but I couldn't really believe it was going to happen."

* * *

About an hour later, as they lay resting on the bed, Gina in an almost foetal position with her bottom tucked into his groin, and his face buried in the softness of her hair, she said, ""I've never made love like that before. You kept finding out the things that make me excited – and doing them."

"That was easy," he replied. "There are so many things that make you excited and every one of them gives me pleasure, too." Then, realizing that his left arm, on which he was lying heavily, was going to sleep he raised himself on one elbow and asked, "Shall we have a drink now, and then see what else we can discover about each other?"

* * *

That evening, after a quick meal of scrambled eggs on toast, one of Dan's limited culinary achievements, they went to the Lyttleton Theatre to see *The Grapes of Wrath* presented by a visiting company from Chicago. Gina shed a few tears, and he agreed that it was a moving performance. On their way

46

back to the Bonnington they talked about theatre, and he promised her more delights later in the week. In the hotel lobby they parted with chaste kisses on cheeks.

* * *

On the warm Saturday evening, after an early meal in Theobalds Road they were walking slowly back to the flat when Gina said, "I'm glad you didn't get theatre tickets for tonight. It's our last evening together and I just want to be with you." Hugging her shoulders tightly, Dan experienced a surge of optimism. His plan for the evening was set fair to succeed.

Once indoors they very quickly started the now familiar routine of preparing to make love. It was almost as if they wanted to recapture the astonishing first discovery of just how hungry each of them was for every small sensation of physical contact. One by one they shed their garments on the living-room floor as with lips and fingers they caressed and stimulated each other. When at last they were completely naked he picked her up and carried her into the bedroom.

The cuckoo clock in the kitchen signalled nine o'clock as they were taking their third intermission, lying side by side on the bed with the duvet thrown on the floor. Slowly and rhythmically Dan's right hand stroked the exquisitely smooth skin of her elevated left buttock. "I want to ask you a very important question," he said. "You don't have to answer it now, if you're not ready but I couldn't let you go home without asking you to think about it."

He felt her muscles tighten beneath his fingers, and she rolled over on to her back. "Have you got to ask me now?" she said, her voice tinged with apprehension.

"I don't want this incredible experience that we've had to be just an interlude for you – for both of us," he said. "I want you to make a decision. Get out of the trap that you're in. Come to London and live with me; and when the technicalities have all been completed – and I know that might take a long time – we'll get married. You can start all over again. We'll both start again, and make something good for each other."

Propping herself up on one elbow Gina looked down at him with troubled eyes. "I was afraid you were going to ask me that," she said. "I want to say yes – I want to more than anything. But I know that I mustn't. I'm fighting a battle. I'm trying to make sure that Bruno will grow up to be a better man than his father, and I can't give up now. Sometimes I think I'm winning, but then Guido will suddenly decide to take him to a football match or motor racing and he'll come back with a completely different attitude towards me. And next week we're going to stay with his grandmother at the beginning of the holidays and I'll have to work hard to stop him being seduced by all her talk about his ancestors and how they were superior to everybody else. I hate the thought of being all on my own again, but I've got to do it."

Dan quickly decided he would have to make do with second best. "Well, if you don't want to make the decision to get away from it all just yet, at least you know that I'll always be waiting for you. Come whenever you can and together we can get away from the loneliness of our everyday life, even if it's only for a week or a fortnight at a time. I'm ready to wait for you for as long as you want me to." He pushed himself up into a sitting position and put his arm around her shoulders.

"It would only make things worse," she said. "Every time I left you I would be thinking of what I was leaving behind – like I'm thinking now – and I'd be dreading what I was having to go back to. And it wouldn't be fair to you, either. You mustn't wait around for something that isn't going to happen. You've been waiting too long. Now you've got to find someone else who will give you what you need – and she'll be lucky when you find her."

She swung her legs over the side of the bed and set off in search of her clothes.

* * *

On their journey to Heathrow next day Gina carefully avoided any reference to the decision she had announced in the bedroom. They talked hopefully about what might be the outcome of the surprise visit by President Botha to Nelson Mandela in jail. Being in a profoundly pessimistic mood, Dan was unable to go along with her belief that it might mark the beginning of the end for apartheid. They were agreed, however, that Boris Becker was likely to be the winner at Wimbledon that afternoon.

It was only when they were about to kiss each other goodbye that she suddenly said, "Please don't write to me Dan. It will only prolong the agony for both of us. You've got to get on with finding somebody else. I'll send you a card at Christmas to say thank you again for the best time of my life; and if you want to you can send one to me. But no letters – I don't want us to keep hoping for something we can't have."

Swiftly and lightly she kissed him on his lips and then she was gone.

CHAPTER SEVEN 18-28 August, 1989

Steeply dramatic mountainsides began to appear through the windows of the train and Dan noticed how his travel companions, seated across the aisle from him, were paying little attention to the splendours of the scenery. They had been here many times before, but for him it was his first excursion into the Bernese Oberland. Already overwhelmed by the grandeur of the distant peaks they had seen from the route along the shore of Lake Thun, he was reluctant to miss a single frame of the changing view on this final stage of the journey, as the railway thrust steeply upward into the heart of the mountains.

It was Ruth who had first discovered the delights of Grindelwald when she was a student in Geneva more than fifty years ago. He had heard the story many times. She had gone back there in 1938, with Daniel, her future husband (though she had stayed chastely with a friend who lived in the village). After he left the Army on his return from Korea it had become an annual pilgrimage for them. Some years later Dan's father and mother had begun to join them on that pilgrimage, when Dan and his sister had become too old to want any longer to take part in a family excursion to Yorkshire, combining a visit to their grandparents with time spent on the beach at Scarborough (beloved by his mother because it was so totally 'unSpanish').

And it had been Ruth who had suggested to Dan that this year he might like to accompany them and discover for himself whatever it was that kept drawing them back to this location on 'the roof of Europe'. With her usual perspicacity she had noticed he was deeply unhappy, even though the Business Awards ceremony had been an outstanding success. He had decided not to tell her about Gina – after all, there was nothing that could be done to alter that situation – but had accepted the invitation to join in their Swiss holiday.

Gradually the sides of the valley widened again and soon he could see a broad horizon of mountain peaks, with to his right a glimpse of the easily recognizable profile of the Eiger. His companions began reaching up for coats and bags stowed on the overhead racks and he knew that they must be approaching their destination.

Their hotel was actually on one of the station platforms. He observed the warm enthusiasm with which his parents and friends were greeted when they passed through the automatic doors into reception, and very soon he had been introduced to several members of staff, who shook him warmly by the hand. A smiling porter, whose accent suggested he might be Italian, or maybe Portuguese, conducted him to his room.

* * *

Muesli was a new experience for Dan and he was enthusiastic about it as he breakfasted with his parents at a table by a window looking out on the station. "I didn't notice that train arriving just now," he remarked. "The double glazing must be very effective."

"The electrified trains are also pretty quiet. It's a great pity British Rail didn't opt for electricity rather than diesel when they started modernizing," said his father.

"Weren't you one of their advisers at that time?" Dan asked.

"No. I was working on road transport. I'll admit to some responsibility for the motorways, but I'm not taking any share in the blame for the neglect of the railways."

Ruth and Daniel appeared, carrying bowls of muesli and glasses of orange juice, and sat down at the next table. Margarita and Arthur greeted them; and Arthur said, "There's an interesting piece in *The Times* about the probability of a non-Communist majority government in Poland. That could really open the floodgates in eastern Europe."

"Have you had a copy of the paper already?" Dan asked his father. "Where did that come from?"

"From the kiosk over there, at the far side of the station," Arthur replied, pointing through the window. "But it's yesterday's paper. They arrive here a day late."

"Any ideas about what you'd like to do today, Dan?" asked Ruth.

"I'd like to have a walk somewhere high up, if that's possible. It looks as if it might be a good day for walking," he replied.

"We're spoilt for choice," said Arthur. "Shall we all go up to First and walk out to the Bachalpsee? The expert picnic-buyers" – he swivelled his head to glance from Ruth to Margarita – "could stop off at the Co-op on the way and get us some lunch to take with us."

"Good idea," said Ruth. "If the weather stays clear it will give you a chance to see the whole valley, Dan. We can point out all the different walks that there are, so that if you would like to walk on your own at any time you can see what there is to choose from."

Dan was happy to agree to this proposal and half-an-hour later they all set out to walk through the village, his companions pointing out to each other changes that had taken place since the previous Autumn. They were upset to discover that the left ear of a stone effigy of a cat that stood outside the Hotel Bellvue had been chipped, and the consensus seemed to be that the damage must have been caused by drunken skiers during the winter sports season. However, they expressed delight at the number of geranium-packed window-boxes still in apparently perfect condition so late in the summer.

Eventually they turned off the main street and up a steep hill to the imposing entrance to the starting-point of the Firstbahn chairlift. "It's the longest chairlift in Europe," Ruth told him. "When we first came here in 1938 it hadn't been built, and now we've heard that it's going to be replaced in a few years' time because the Swiss have strict rules about how old a chairlift can be. They're going to replace it with 'gondolas' – little closed-in cabins instead of the open seats."

"It's tempting to say that the younger generation aren't up to facing the elements unprotected, but I suppose it may well suit us better in our old age," said Daniel. "By the way, Dan, you'll get a half-fare reduction on it with your travel card. That works for nearly every form of transport, and not just the railways."

Since the chairlift seats were in pairs Dan travelled up on his own, with Daniel and Ruth ahead of him on the cable, and beyond them his parents. Many times in the past he had heard descriptions of what an exhilarating ride it was, from his mother and before that from Ruth. Ruth, he remembered, had told him how nervous she had felt on the first occasion, and how she had made up a little song to distract her thoughts. As they approached the half-way station at Bort he heard her singing, with Daniel joining in, and beyond them he was sure he could just detect the voices of his parents. The nonsense rhyme came floating back to him on the breeze:

> *The kindly men of Oberhaus,*
> *The merry men of Egg,*
> *And Berghaus Bort, Berghaus Bort,*
> *Doing what he berghaus ort.*

When they arrived at the First terminus he was worried that the bar across the front of his seat might not open, but a moderate tug was enough to release it and he stepped down while the seat moved away behind him.

"I thought we would see some cows below us, but the meadows were empty," he said as he rejoined his friends.

"At this time of year the cows are as high up as they can go," said Daniel. "You'll see some of them very shortly."

They moved out of the terminal building into bright sunshine. A small group of Japanese were taking photographs and a white haired couple were helping one another to fasten large haversacks on their backs. In the middle distance he could see a group of about a dozen people walking in single file along a path on the mountainside, and above them was a grazing herd of cattle.

Dan was shown the restaurant and gift shop beside the *sesselbahn* station, and then they set out on their walk. It took him some time to get his bearings because every bend in the path seemed to open up yet another breathtaking view. On either side of the path there were clumps of flowers to be identified; and before long a piercing whistle revealed the presence of a family of marmots. There was something, too, about the quality of the air in his lungs that induced a feeling of relaxation.

After about an hour's walking they arrived at a surprisingly large lake and there, with some difficulty, they sought out a grassy mound that was level enough to sit on and have their picnic lunch. The main course was tangy *Bernerkäse* with several varieties of bread rolls, and there were bananas and apricots (Italian) to follow. Dan was introduced to a refreshing soft drink called 'Rivella', reputedly brimful of health-giving Swiss ingredients.

On the walk back to First Margarita suddenly exclaimed "Eagle!" and pointed up towards the ridge on their left. Just above the skyline he could see a very large bird hovering, and when Daniel lent him his binoculars he was able to make out the tawny plumage of a golden eagle. One of the marmot sentries must have seen it simultaneously, for there was a loud whistle and halfway up the ridge they glimpsed a couple of furry brown bodies disappearing into a hole in the ground.

On the chairlift going down to the village his mother sat beside him and asked how he was enjoying the mountains. Glancing at his bare forearm, where his sleeve was rolled up, she asked, "Is that spot a return of the old psoriasis? I thought you'd managed to get it all cleared up a couple of years ago."

"Yes, I did – apart from the occasional spot on my scalp, beneath the hair. But I'm afraid there have been some signs of recurrence on my arms and my chest in the last month," he replied. "Since it's allegedly in the genes I suppose it never completely goes away."

"I hope you don't have as much of it as you did last time," she said. "I know you were able to keep it covered up, but in the end you had to go into hospital to get rid of it. If it starts getting worse this time maybe you should have the treatment sooner rather than later."

"Well, I'm hoping it's just going to be a few spots; and maybe all this wonderful sunshine will help me to get rid of it. I remember last time round my doctor told me he once had a psoriasis patient who went by sea to Australia, and by the time they were through the Suez Canal the psoriasis had gone. But if the symptoms should get any worse I'll have a word with the doctor, though I know the hospital won't take me in for treatment unless it becomes pretty extensive, like it did before.

"Oh, look! There are a couple of little deer on the edge of the trees," he exclaimed, glad to have an opportunity to move the conversation away from his skin complaint – and from any questioning by his mother of what might have caused it to break out at this particular time.

* * *

In the week that followed Dan sometimes accompanied his family on outings, observing that age did not seem greatly to have impeded their ability to keep pace with him, although they assured him they were no longer undertaking the distances they had once enjoyed. His father suggested he might like to tackle the challenge of an all-day walk along the northern skyline, from First to Schynigge Platte, but he decided to leave that for a future visit, when his legs might have become more accustomed to the mountains.

His first solo expedition was on the Monday, when the others planned to visit a friend first met by Ruth in her student days, who lived in the village. Her husband, who had also become a friend to them all, had died of cancer only four months ago. He set out well briefed in advance and carrying a map obtained from the friendly and efficient tourist office. (None of the others had bothered to bring a map since every route in the region was firmly etched in their memories.)

The first stage of his journey was in the bright yellow local bus that followed a zig-zagging road up the mountainside to terminate at Bussalp, a berghaus restaurant on the lip of a huge tilted saucer of alpine meadows below the peak of the Faulhorn. Well advised by his family, he sat at a wooden table outside the restaurant, drinking hot chocolate and marvelling at the breathtaking view across the valley to the Eiger and the Lower Glacier. And then he set out on his walk by a well-signposted path that wound its way along the flank of the mountain ridge, across alpine pasture into forest and then out again into grassland where herds of cows were grazing, and back again into forest. Eventually it passed a couple of chalets and crossed a rushing stream, bringing him into sight of the familiar chairlift on which he had travelled two days before.

As he sat outside the Berghaus Bort eating a huge plateful of *Rösti mit Ei* he remembered Ruth's crazy little song. At the next table sat a young couple – Swiss he guessed, from overhearing snatches of conversation in an almost unintelligible version of German – who seemed totally absorbed in one another. Looking at their happy faces he realized just how intensely he wanted to be sharing this experience with someone else – someone who would look into his eyes with that blend of intimacy and expectation he could see in the face of the young woman. He wondered if they were on their honeymoon, or possibly at an even earlier stage in their relationship.

When he had paid the buxom waitress, who wished him "a nice day" in English, he walked across to the Firstbahn Station and floated over pasture and woodland, streams and chalets, back down to the village.

* * *

In the days that followed Dan accompanied his family on walks across the Grosse Scheidegg and the Kleine Scheidegg which bounded the western and eastern ends of the valley, each opening up immense new vistas of mountain ranges stretching in either direction. And on Saturday, when the weather outlook was doubtful, they descended by train to Interlaken and walked along the shore of Lake Brienz to the charming village of Bönigen. From there they took a paddle steamer to Brienz, where he marvelled at the skill of the local woodcarvers.

Expeditions on his own included a walk down from Kleine Sheidegg, base for climbers of the Eiger, along the flank of the Jungfrau to the village of Wengen, traversing the route of the celebrated Lauberhorn ski race, now long clear of snow and covered in summer vegetation. Glimpses of roe deer and red squirrels in the woods, and marmots and chamois on the alps, enlivened his walk. The following day he walked down from Grosse Scheidegg, stopping for lunch of Alpine cheese and salad at the Schwarzwaldalp berghaus, to the Reichenbach Falls, where the fate of Sherlock Holmes was still attracting the tourists. Farther down, in the small town of Meiringen, he was surprised to discover a street sign saying 'Baker Street'. It would seem that the town was not content to be celebrated only for the invention of the meringue.

* * *

When at last they boarded the BOB train to begin their return journey to London Daniel asked him, "Do you think this is a place you'll come back to one day?"

"I know from what you've all told me that I've only just begun to discover it," he replied. "So I'm sure I'll be back before very long. You've really whetted my appetite for the Oberland."

As he slung his rucksack on to the overhead rack he felt his shirt catch on the back of his left shoulder. Exploring it with his fingertips he could feel the presence of another small plaque of psoriasis. So the sunshine and the mountain air hadn't, after all, effected a cure. He would need to pay a visit to his doctor when he got home.

CHAPTER EIGHT 10 to 15 November, 1989

Ruth had come to visit Dan in hospital because on the following day she and Daniel would be travelling to America. They were going to combine a holiday with book-signings requested by their publishers: Ruth in Boston and Daniel in New York.

"I'm very lucky to have been given this side room," said Dan, as he ushered her to the single chair and sat down facing her on the side of the bed. "Because the ward is primarily for dermatology they don't often have patients who need to be isolated, and so when I said I'd like to get on with some paperwork while I'm in here they very kindly let me have one of the two side rooms. Though I don't actually have as much time to myself as I thought I might it's still been very useful – particularly when I'm talking to visitors from the office."

"What are the other patients like?" Ruth asked. "I noticed as I came through that they all seemed to be out of bed and looking fairly active."

"They're a pretty mixed bunch, but we get along well together. Several of them are quite elderly. Alfred is a veteran of the War and a bit of an Ancient Mariner. He would happily talk for hours. Served in Italy and had a spell as an orderly at Alexander's HQ; so he might even have encountered Daniel. And we have one woman, Betty Sanders, who's in the other side room. She told me her psoriasis began soon after she was dug out of the wreckage of her home in Bermondsey during the Blitz. She was a teenager at the time. A chap who's just a bit younger – probably late fifties – called Ken Belcrow has been a cameraman in films and TV, but I think he's been out of work for some time. Those are the ones I've got to know best so far; but I've only been here four days. A couple of younger chaps left today and their beds are still empty. We all get together at a long table for meals and one tends to talk to the people who are closest."

"And what about the staff? Are they treating you well?"

"I'd met my consultant before. Professor Vernon was in charge when I had the treatment eight years ago. But I've seen him only once. He prescribed what ought to be done to me and then Doctor Anson took over.

He's a registrar, I think. Very pleasant chap. But it's the nurses who do the actual work – anointing me and wrapping bits of me in gauze, and then rubbing it all off again before I have my bath every morning. So far I've had two different ones. There's a staff nurse called Kathy Barrington who really knows what she's doing and is very gentle. And there's a younger nurse whose name is Bennett and who doesn't seem to be so well trained. I've had to point things out to her a few times. One of the night nurses, Tessa King, is very friendly. Last night I was doing some writing till quite late and she asked if I'd like to have some toast – which I did. She was making it for herself and her colleague. In the morning I helped her to make the beds. She taught me how to do 'hospital corners'."

"It sounds as if you've really settled in," said Ruth. "How much longer do you expect to be here?"

"Professor Vernon said he thought they could get me clear in a fortnight, but Doctor Anson was a bit more cautious. Fortunately I haven't got any important engagements till the beginning of December. Oh, you'll be amused to know that I have become a pin-up. Professor Vernon said my 'plaques' were such a classic example of psoriasis that he'd like to have me photographed for teaching purposes. So now the hospital has a full frontal slide of me in the nude, and another of my back. Fame at last."

Ruth laughed. "You'll soon have a fan club wanting your autograph," she said.

"Fortunately I don't think my face is included in the picture. By the way, have you seen that fantastic photo in *The Times* today – people knocking down the Wall in Berlin?"

"Yes, isn't it incredible? Daniel was quite moved when he opened the paper at breakfast. He said it made him feel that all the work he did when they were setting up NATO had been worthwhile. But I'm afraid a lot of younger people are going to forget about that and assume that this was something that was inevitable – bound to happen sooner or later."

"You could be right there," said Dan. "This morning when Nurse Bennett was removing my ointment, not very gently, she said, 'Isn't it good they're able to start knocking down that wall they built to keep out the Communists?' At least I was able to do a little bit of educating. I told her about the time I came through Checkpoint Charlie a couple of years ago and watched the Stasi looking underneath the bus to make sure some poor soul wasn't trying to escape by hanging on to the axle. I hope the Wall comes down, but I hope it will never be forgotten. It's the ultimate symbol of what happens when utopian idealists try to create a paradise on earth where everybody is going to be equal."

Ruth nodded her head. "Daniel thinks the symbolism is so powerful that this might be the moment to start reforming the UN and trying to make it into what it was originally intended to be. Symbolism can have the effect of making people think new thoughts."

"A bit like Wordsworth's first reaction to the French Revolution," said Dan. *"Bliss was it in that dawn to be alive...* But it didn't turn out in the way he thought it would."

"Maybe the reason for that was in his second line: *And to be young was very heaven,"* said Ruth. "The people who determined what actually happened were not the young. They were older, and they brought all their existing baggage to the party. This time it's your generation who are going to be the key players, and I hope they're going to get it right."

"I think the real decision-makers may be just a few years older than me," said Dan. "Getting to the top in politics takes a long time these days – no more William Pitt the Younger. But I know what you mean. We're the ones who could influence the decision-makers if we tried hard enough. The problem is that the sort of sensible ideas Daniel is proposing don't make for headline-grabbing policies. They could be a lot more important than the rate of income tax but there are no votes in them."

There was a tap on the door and a lean-faced, middle-aged man put his head around it and said, "Kathy is making tea. Would you like a cup – and one for the lady?"

When the offer had been accepted and he had gone to fetch the tea Dan said, "That was Ken, the cameraman. He's a good chap but I think under-employment is getting to him and sapping his morale. Yesterday Doctor Anson was talking to me about the danger of patients becoming institutionalised and he said 'I think poor old Ken is a bit at risk.' Considering how little time he's able to spend with any one patient I think

Anson is very perceptive. In general I'm quite impressed by the medical staff, but I think the nurses could benefit from a bit more supervision. Some of them are excellent, but there are times when nobody seems to be in charge, and cleanliness in the ward for example leaves a lot to be desired."

"I think it was a great mistake to abolish the post of matron," said Ruth. "The Hattie Jacques image was a bit of a caricature but they really did do an important job."

"My guess is that one day they'll be brought back again," said Dan. "This ward may not be a high-risk zone, but it would only need an outbreak of some dirt-based infection in more vulnerable areas and the scandal would panic the politicians and have them reaching for the obvious solution."

"In the meantime I'm sure you'll do your best to give the nurses some tactful guidance," said Ruth, smiling. "I think I really should be going now. There's a heck of a lot of packing still to be done and I hate leaving it to the last minute. I hope by the time we return you'll be out and striding around with an unblemished skin, like you were the last time. I'll send a postcard from the States to your office address, so that you'll be sure to get it quickly."

As she closed the door behind her Dan remembered how when he had first, at around the age of fifteen, thought about the possibility of being married he had said to himself, 'I want to marry somebody like Aunty Ruth – only with black hair like Mam.'

* * *

It was Monday morning and Dan was aware that a new group of nurses had taken over on the ward. A short, middle-aged staff nurse called Gloria Mendoza helped him with removing the dressings and ointment and having a bath. He learnt that she was from the Philippines and had been in Britain for thirteen years. It wasn't until after lunchtime that she was able to apply his new treatment, and while she was doing it they chatted.

"Are you still in touch with family in the Philippines?" he asked.

"Over there and here too," she replied. "I have two cousins, both working as nurses. One is at the Royal Marsden and the other is in Luton. I have a brother back home but he doesn't write very often. My mother died five years ago."

"And your father?" he asked, as she fastened a swathe of surgical gauze around his trunk.

"My father was killed by the Japanese. He hid some rice for the family when they said he had to give them everything he'd harvested, and one of our neighbours betrayed him. They killed him – with bayonets because they said they didn't want to waste bullets. I was too small at the time to understand what had happened but my mother told me about it later on."

"It must have been a terrible time for your mother," he said, struggling to imagine the situation.

"She had to be tough. I remember when the news was on the radio that the Americans had dropped the big bomb on Japan she went out in the street with everyone else to dance and sing. I think it must have been soon afterwards that she told me what had happened to my father."

* * *

On the following afternoon Anne, his PA, came to visit, bearing a folder full of letters to be signed, and a Terry's Chocolate Orange, to which she knew he was partial. As he worked his way through the letters she said, "We've had some bumph about the 'Small States Conference on Sea Level Rise' that's happening this week. Is it something that might interest our journalists – the ones who weren't lucky enough to get sent to the Maldives to cover it?"

"That's a good possibility. Have a look through the names to see who's attending from here and give me a ring tomorrow. There's probably somebody from the Commonwealth Secretariat who could give journalists a balanced assessment of whatever they decide. The sensational bits about how countries are going to disappear off the map will get picked up instantly by the media, but we could arrange a lunchtime meeting to discuss whatever practical proposals may come out of the conference."

He handed back the folder and asked, "How is John getting on with the plans for the sixth-form competition?"

"Oh, he asked me to tell you that he's completed a draft of the publicity leaflet and he'd like to bring it in tomorrow afternoon for you to have a look at."

"That'll be fine; but ask him not to come before three o'clock, just in case they haven't managed to do my treatment before lunch."

"Aren't the nurses very efficient, then?"

"Most of them are; but it's more a problem of having sometimes to deal with the unexpected. That must be inevitable in a hospital. And I'm not high on the list of timetable priorities – which is understandable."

* * *

The next day his treatment was actually done early. A new staff nurse, accompanied by a student nurse, took over from the night shift and immediately everything seemed to be moving at a faster pace – but in a mood of genial briskness that before long had everyone smiling. The staff nurse was not only efficient but she was also, Daniel thought, the most beautiful woman he had ever seen. She was a little under average height, and her broad red belt formed a tiny frontier between two zones of anatomical perfection. (Later on he did notice that her calves were a little on the slender side.) But it was her face that really captivated him. Her cheek-bones were high and suggestive of the Orient while her lips were almost African in their fullness, but her nose was straight and Indo-European. The light brown colour of her skin could easily have been mistaken for a successful suntan. Her black eyes under arched brows seemed to sparkle with perpetual good humour, while a set of gleaming white teeth enhanced the smiles that within minutes had everyone in the ward adoring her.

Dan discovered before long that the new nurse's name was Dorcas Lee, but it was not until she arrived in his room with the dithranol paste, spatulas, surgical gauze and scissors on a tray to do his treatment that he was able to discover more about her. As she very gently applied the paste they

63

talked about how long he had been in the ward and about the progress of his treatment. When it came to covering affected areas with gauze to keep the paste in place she surprised him by instructing him to place his wrists underneath her armpits while she secured a broad band of gauze around his trunk. Emboldened by physical proximity he asked, "What part of the world do you come from?"

She smiled quizzically. "Where do you think?"

"Well, the place where I've seen more beautiful women than anywhere else is Trinidad, so that would be my guess."

"You're partly right," she said, sounding surprised. "My father was from Trinidad and I went to college there, but I was born and grew up in Saint Lucia, which is my mother's country."

"I spent a very happy year in Saint Lucia when I left university, but I was teaching in a secondary school and you would still have been in primary school then. Otherwise I might have met you," he said, "and I'm sure I would have noticed you."

"I expect you'd like to know what went into my mixture," she said, starting to tidy up.

"I certainly would, if you don't mind telling me."

She smiled. "Well, you seem to like the result. My father's father was a sailor from Shanghai and he married an Indian girl in Trinidad and settled there, and that's where my father was born, and his two sisters. He became a sailor, too, and worked on a banana boat. The boat used to call at Castries to pick up the bananas and take them to England. He met my mother at church on Sunday – they'd both been brought up as Baptists – and, unlike a lot of sailors, he married her, even though he went on sailing."

Dan began putting on his shirt and trousers as she continued: "My mother's father was English. She once told me his name was Mackintosh; so maybe he was actually Scottish. Apparently he left Saint Lucia before Mammy was born, but he gave her mother some money before he went. Granny was Afro-Caribbean, and they say she was very beautiful when she was young."

"I think all your forebears must have been pretty good-looking to produce an end result like you," said Dan, adding quickly, so as not to labour the flattery, "Did you see much of your father when you were growing up?"

"He died in an accident at sea when I was only three and my brother, Matthew, was less than a year old. Mammy had a hard time bringing us up. I owe her an awful lot. When you're a kid you don't realize what it's costing to give you little things that you take for granted – and big things, too. After we left home she was promoted to be manager of the shop where she worked, and she's still doing that job. Are your parents still alive?"

"Yes; they'll be coming in to see me tomorrow afternoon. If you're around I'll introduce you. My mother is Spanish – so I'm a mixture, too, though I don't have as many ingredients as you do."

"That explains it," she said, sitting down on the edge of the bed. "When I first saw you I thought you didn't look English. Do you spend much time in Spain?"

"No. My mother was a refugee from the Civil War and she had no desire to go back there. I've been to Spain to see what it's like but I much prefer Italy, when I have the time to travel."

There was a tap on the door and Sylvia, the student nurse, put her head around it and said, "Mrs Sanders' tablets haven't come from the pharmacy. What should I do?"

"I'll be right with you," said Dorcas, standing up and taking the treatment tray from the bedside table. "We mustn't allow Mrs Sanders to start getting anxious. See you later alligator."

"In a while crocodile," Dan replied.

* * *

Dan had no opportunity to resume the conversation until next morning, when she came once again to his room to remove the dithranol paste before he had his bath. As she snipped the gauze dressings he said, "You must have the smallest waist in the hospital. What is it – twenty-two inches?"

"Actually it's twenty-one," she replied, "but then I'm not very tall."

"Apart from height I would think your dimensions meet the standard 'beauty queen' requirements – or even better. Have you ever thought of entering for a contest?"

"When I was a student in Trinidad some people tried to persuade me, but I didn't want the hassle. And if my mother had got to hear about it she would have been very upset. Nowadays, of course, I'm much too old for that kind of thing. I think twenty-one is just about 'over the hill' for beauty contests."

"I can't believe you were more beautiful at twenty-one than you are now," he said, turning his head to look into her eyes.

She returned his glance evenly, saying, "Flattery will get you nowhere. Pass me the scissors please."

As she removed the dressings from his forearms she remarked "There's a little bit of burning on your left arm but everywhere else seems to be clear."

"That's good. On Sunday I had quite a lot on my back and chest, and my temperature went up to over a hundred. Being Sunday, of course, there was no doctor around, but Sister had a look at me and told me to keep drinking water. So that's what I did, and the temperature came down after about three hours. I think Sally had been a bit heavy-handed when she applied the treatment on Saturday."

"Well, I think you'll agree that I'm not heavy-handed," said Dorcas. "If you can have a fairly quick bath I'll be able to do your treatment before lunchtime – but be sure to have a good soak for at least ten minutes."

Delighted at the prospect of a second encounter with her, Dan readily agreed to be quick in the bathroom. When the last dressing had been removed from his leg he said, "I'd better cover my nakedness on the way to the bath or I might give Mrs Sanders a nasty shock." And he took down his dressing-gown from the peg on the back of the door.

"You never know – Betty might be glad of the thrill. It could be a long time since she last had one," said Dorcas, as he picked up his towel and prepared to leave.

For once he didn't linger in the relaxing warmth, and coal-tar aroma, of the bath; and his attempts to think of a conversational opening that might take the relationship to a more intimate level were unsuccessful. As he walked back through the ward he signalled to Dorcas. She was chatting to Alfred, who had had no visitors that day. When she arrived in his room a few minutes later he was stripped and ready to be 'plastered'.

"Poor old Alfred is very cross with his family because they don't come to see him more often," she said. "He has two sons and a daughter and I don't know how many grandchildren, all living around London, but they don't seem to talk to each other about their visiting, and those who do come all seem to arrive at the same time on Sunday afternoon. He's a widower and I think he gets very lonely." She put the treatment tray on the bedside table and opened the pot of dithranol paste. "I don't want to hurry this and then risk sending up your temperature again if I let some of the paste get on to your good skin."

As she stepped behind him to begin work on his back he turned his head to look at her and said, "Paste on the skin isn't the only thing that can send up my temperature."

"What do you mean?" she asked.

"Well, for example, those stockings you're wearing…"

"Stockings? How do you know they're not tights?"

"When you were sitting on Alfred's bed you crossed your legs and I experienced a distinct rise in temperature."

"You should keep your eyes to yourself," she said, and gave him a light smack on his right buttock.

He chuckled and then, to his astonishment, realized that he was having an erection. Rapidly he moved his hands to conceal what was happening, but his very action may have alerted her to the event, for she said, "You should know that I blush, just like you do, only you can't see it because of the colour of my skin."

Keeping his hands in place he replied, "And you must know, because you've studied anatomy, that I'm not in conscious control of what happens down there. I would never deliberately try to embarrass you, but I'm afraid Carlos is a little less considerate."

To his great relief she laughed. "Why do you call him Carlos?"

"That's my middle name – from my Spanish grandfather – and he's in the middle of me, sort of. I'm not saying he's more Spanish than the rest of me. I think we're all the same below the belt."

"Actually I'm not," she said. "From my waist down my skin is darker than on the top half of me. It's something that happens occasionally in people of… mixed ethnicity."

"I've never heard of that," said Dan, and after a moment's hesitation he added, "I hope maybe one day I'll have an opportunity to see just how much difference there is."

"Now you're making me blush again," she complained.

Sensing an opportunity to move the relationship forward, he said, "Because I've caused you embarrassment – even though it wasn't intentional – I think I ought to make it up to you. When I've stopped being your patient, which I hope will happen next week, would you allow me to take you to lunch – or dinner if you prefer? I know they don't give you a lot of time off, but we could plan it to fit in with your timetable."

"Oh, what a brilliant idea!" she said, and he thought she meant it. "Actually you don't really owe me anything, because I was the one who… made the first move. But I'd love to have a chance to talk properly without being interrupted. You've found out quite a lot about me but I don't really know much about you. It would give me a chance to find out your secrets, if you have any."

"We all have secrets," said Dan. "That's what makes us interesting. Let's find a date when we can do some swapping."

"I'll check my diary when I go off shift this evening," she said. "Now, put your hands under my oxters and we'll get the big dressing on."

CHAPTER NINE 23 November, 1989

The high-backed benches facing one another like the seating in a railway compartment gave a sense of privacy, Daniel thought as he watched Dorcas scanning the dinner menu in his favourite restaurant. He hoped that their conversation was going to be an intimate one, even though she was now formally dressed in a dark green jacket and skirt with a high-necked cream-coloured blouse, in contrast to their last encounter, when she was wearing her uniform and he was wearing nothing at all.

They gave their orders to Giovanni, who shot a glance at Dan over the top of his note-pad that indicated plainly, but discreetly, how impressed he was by the beauty of his dinner-guest.

While they waited for the minestrone soup to arrive Dan enquired about what had been happening in the ward and was regaled with accounts of a couple of small but amusing mishaps involving misunderstood choices from the menu. "Actually the food was much better than I thought it was going to be," he said, "but not in the same class as what we are about to receive."

"When you were little did you use those words at home to say grace?" she asked.

"What words?" he responded, puzzled by her question.

"For what we are about to receive may the Lord make us truly thankful."

"Oh yes, I have heard them," he replied, laughing, "but at school, not at home. We weren't a religious family, though my grandmother was a bit that way. She sang in a church choir, in York."

"My Mammy is very religious. We went to church twice every Sunday. She's a good person, and going to church seems to make her happy, but it gives her some weird ideas. She brought me up to believe that every word in the Bible was true, and if you didn't believe that you'd go to hell."

"When did you start having doubts about that – or did you?" he asked.

70

"At school we were taught about dinosaurs and how they'd lived millions of years ago, and I thought that was funny, because in Sunday School I'd been told that the world was only about six thousand years old. I asked Mammy about it, and she said that God had put dinosaurs bones in the ground to test people's faith. They had to choose between believing the Bible or believing the scientists; and if they believed the scientists they'd go to hell. Don't get me wrong – Mammy is a really kind, friendly sort of person. She just happens to believe in a god who invented hell so that people would know there was a really good reason for not being bad. She used to say that if more people believed in hell we wouldn't need to have a police force."

"Unfortunately that didn't work even in the days when most people did believe in hell – or said they did," said Dan, "but evidence isn't something that's allowed to get in the way of belief. If it was there wouldn't be any religions."

"I know. Something else that started to bother me around that time was the fact that most of my school friends were Roman Catholics, and our Baptist Pastor, Mr Mullen, taught us that Catholics couldn't go to heaven because they hadn't accepted the Lord Jesus Christ as their personal saviour, and so it was our duty to try and convert them. He used to preach at open-air meetings. He was actually an American, from Alabama."

"It's possible that I have seen one of those meetings," said Dan. "I remember once when I was walking across Columbus Square I saw a little group of people who were singing very loudly, and it was a hymn in English. I stopped to listen because it was a hymn I had sung at school – *All things bright and beautiful*."

Dorcas smiled and softly sang the second line in a rich contralto voice: *All creatures great and small*.

"That was something else that used to bother me," she went on. "The Lord God might have made them all, but he'd also made all the stupid, nasty creatures, like mosquitos and snakes."

"Now there you've hit on a conundrum that has given rise to whole libraries of books. But you must have been a very thoughtful little girl."

"I suppose that's what happens if you're brought up by religious people," she said. "You either go along with it and sing the happy choruses or you start thinking about the things that don't add up. But I stopped being serious when I got to Trinidad."

The minestrone soup arrived and occupied their attention for the next few minutes. Then Dan, in search of more background information, asked, "Did you enjoy your student days in Trinidad?"

"Most of the time I did, but actually religion popped its ugly head up again. I started going out with an Indian medical student, a lovely guy called Raj. His family were Hindus but he didn't believe any of the religious stuff, and I used to tease him about having all those gods with elephant heads or four arms. And I remember he said once, "Well, the Christians have two gods and a ghost, and some of them have a blessed virgin as well." His father was a Brahmin and made the whole family go to the temple when they had their special festivals, like Diwali and Navarathi and Holi. But he said his father didn't actually believe in the supernatural stuff. According to him it was just the way their ancestors had tried to explain how the world worked in times when they didn't have the tools to help them discover what was really going on. But he believed the rituals and the festivals helped to give them a feeling for who they were and where they'd come from."

"Did you ever meet his father?"

"No. Raj finished his houseman year at the 'General' – he'd done his training in Barbardos – and became a GP; and then he made his mother happy by marrying a nice Indian girl."

"Was that when you decided to come to Britain?"

She gave him a wry smile and nodded her head. "There are times when the past… sort of lets you down and it's best to move on to something completely new – don't you think?"

"I know exactly what you mean," he said, smiling. "When I… got my divorce I decided I ought to move to a different job. I'd been earning quite a lot of money by giving advice to people who didn't really want it, but were told by other people that they needed it. Some of them were in Trinidad, as it happens. Then, by good luck, my present job came along, and I took it."

Giovanni cleared away the empty soup plates and carefully brushed some ciabatta crumbs from the tablecloth. Dorcas was having ravioli and he had decided on tortellini. "I'd like to try more Italian dishes," she said. "Do you know, I've never eaten spaghetti."

"I like spaghetti, but it's not something you can eat in company and keep your dignity," he said.

Dorcas grinned mischievously. "I thought I'd be the last person you'd try to keep your dignity with. It went a long time ago, didn't it?"

"You could say that," he replied. "Anyhow, here comes your ravioli."

For a few minutes they concentrated on their plates. Then Dan asked, "Did you enjoy living in Trinidad?"

"What I enjoyed most was getting away from home. Don't get me wrong. I love my Mammy and she did a terrific job, bringing up Matthew and me all on her own. But the school and the neighbours and the church – the church most of all – was starting to make me feel… kind of shut into something that was never going to change. I thought when I got to Trinidad I'd be moving into a big new world."

"And did it work out like that?"

"Not exactly. The best bit was being able to start thinking for myself, and realizing that a lot of the stuff I'd been told was important was just the opinions of people who didn't know very much at all about the world. Port of Spain was different, but it wasn't exactly New York or London. I wanted to find out more about culture – pictures and history and music and books – but there wasn't all that much, unless you happen to like steel bands. Did you ever look in the museum there? It was so dull and dusty, and it seemed to be all about Trinidad. I wanted to find out about the rest of the world. It wasn't that much better when I went to Leeds – though the City Art Gallery's not bad, and they have a music festival, but it's only every three years. That's why I decided to move to London, even though the Leeds hospital was a good one and I enjoyed working there."

"And has London lived up to your expectations?"

"Oh yes. But I'm only just starting to find out how much there is to see and do. When I first got here I rushed around in my spare time, going to the National Gallery and the British Museum and Westminster Abbey and the Festival Hall. It was very exciting, but then I realized I wasn't taking in very much and I'd got to slow down and be a bit more… systematic."

Her enthusiasm surprised Dan, and he asked, "Do you have any priorities?"

"I think I want to find out more about how all the different people in the world got to be the way they are now. As you know, I got my genes from a lot of different places. Raj told me quite a bit about India, even though he'd never been there himself, but I don't know anything about China or Africa. And when I was a kid I had to read about all those other people in the Bible – the Egyptians and the Assyrians and the Romans. The people who wrote the Bible didn't like them but they usually seemed to be running the show in those days and I'd like to know who they were and what happened to them."

"That's a pretty ambitious wish list," said Dan, "and London's probably about the best place you could be in to find out at least a little bit about all of them. Oddly enough, next week I'm going to be chairing a committee meeting that's concerned with very much the same subject."

"Is that connected with your work. I thought that was all about economics."

"No. It's something I do in my spare time. Actually I don't do a great deal these days, apart from chairing the committee, but I helped to set up the organization a long time ago. In a way it started in St Lucia. I was teaching there, as I told you, even though I'm not a trained teacher, and I discovered that most of the kids knew very little about what had happened in the past outside their own island, and maybe in Britain. When I got back here I talked to a friend from university called Wilfred Tike, who had started working as a history teacher. He said he'd got the impression that most kids in Britain were also being given a very narrow view of history. They were taught maybe about the Second World War and then about Henry VIII, and after that they stopped learning history.

"Anyhow, we had a number of conversations and started involving other friends of his from the time when he was studying at the Institute of Education. Eventually I suggested we should try to set up a network for people who shared our concern and wanted to do something about it. And that was how the World History Education Network – WHEN for short – came into existence."

"And you're the chairman of its committee?"

"Yes. It was all very informal to begin with. We wrote articles for professional journals and circulated draft syllabuses for various age levels. Then we decided, since it was world history we were talking about, we should try to involve some people from other countries. We thought about advertising, but that was going to involve money and we didn't have any funds. So we thought we'd do some fundraising; but we had to reassure people that we were a serious, responsible organization that would make good use of their money. I thought of an old friend I used to play with when we were both in short trousers and who happens to be a viscount. So I asked Leo if he would become our President and let us use his name on our headed notepaper and he agreed, because he was genuinely interested in what we were doing. It worked like a dream. Several trusts agreed to talk to us, and a couple of publishers, and in about a year we were able to have a paid secretary; and now we have members in nine countries – including Barbados."

"I've noticed that English people are still a bit snobby about titles," said Dorcas. "It was great that it worked out for you."

"The irony of it is that Leo is the least snobbish of people. I remember having a long chat with him when he was agonizing about whether he should take his seat in the House of Lords and start using the title. His father was killed in the War when he was still a baby. Several of his closest friends – and I was one of them – persuaded him that being in the Lords would give him a platform to work for things he believed in very strongly. And that's how it has actually worked. He sits as a Crossbencher, which means he doesn't belong to any of the political parties."

"What made you feel so strongly about world history that you actually started an organization?" Dorcas asked.

"Apart from the experience I had with kids in St Lucia, I think it was the way I was grabbed by it myself when I was a youngster. I think it must have been my tenth birthday when my parents gave me a book called the *Oxford Junior Encyclopaedia*. I was already interested in British history by that time and I knew the names of all the battles and the kings and the famous men. Then I opened the book and read about the Sumerians and realized there was a whole world of history still waiting to be discovered. Here were these people who'd invented the wheel and had been the first to divide the day into twenty-four hours, with sixty minutes to the hour, and I'd never heard of them before. And then I turned back some pages and came across the incredible things the Chinese had been up to long before England had come into existence.

"It was very exciting for a schoolboy, discovering a story with an endless cast of characters and a plot that was always changing. But later on, when I'd learned a lot more, I realized that knowing at least the fundamental facts of history was essential if you wanted to understand how we'd managed to get from being apes to being astronauts – and where we might be going next."

Dorcas used a crust of ciabatta to mop up the surplus sauce on her plate. "I know so little. Maybe you could recommend one or two good books to get started with," she said.

"Better than that – I can lend you one I think would be ideal to start with. It was given to me by one of my aunts when she heard I was interested, and it was written by someone who'd been a colleague of hers when she worked in the BBC during the War, a man called Gombrich who was a refugee from Austria."

"Brilliant! Thank you very much. I think if I know a bit more about the facts then things I'm looking at, in the British Museum, for example, will make more sense to me."

"Maybe we could look at some things together," he suggested. "If you'd like it I know I'd enjoy being able to see things through your eyes as well as my own."

"Oh, that's a super idea," she exclaimed, and he thought she really meant it.

Giovanni enquired if they would have some *dolci*, and Dan suggested they have the tiramisu, saying, "Every restaurant seems to have its own version but I can recommend Giovanni's tiramisu from long experience."

"Do you eat here often, then?" Dorcas asked when the restauranter had left them.

"Quite often. It's not far from where I live, and though I do sometimes have a solitary meal in front of the telly – and I'm a reasonable cook – I prefer eating in company."

"I don't often cook for myself though, of course, Mammy taught me how to do it," said Dorcas. "But my flatmate, Helen, and I are hardly ever at home at the same time, and my spare time is so precious, I prefer to use it in other ways."

"Do you often go to the theatre?" he asked.

"I like it, but it's a bit expensive."

"I enjoy the theatre more when I have someone to share it with," he said. "Would you like to come with me some time – if we can find a date that will fit in with your timetable?"

"I can see that my name's going to start appearing in your diary," she said, giving him a sideways glance. "I'd love to – specially because you're going to be paying. You must have found Castries a bit boring in the evenings."

"I did until I met Catherine, the girl who later became my wife. She was also there with VSO."

Dorcas paused for a moment, evidently uncertain whether or not to make a joke, and then said, "Oh well, I'm sure you must have found plenty to do after that."

"We did," he replied; and then the tiramisu arrived.

They had begun to sip their coffee when Dorcas looked at the tiny silver watch on her wrist and said, "This has been a really super evening but tomorrow morning is one of my early ones and I think I should soon be going home."

"It would never do if breakfast was late in the ward," he responded, "and if some poor sod who'd been looking forward to having you do his treatment thought you might not be coming after all. May I walk you home? I know your flat isn't very far away."

Dorcas said she'd be happy to have his company. As they crossed over Guildford Street and into dimly-lit Lansdowne Terrace he felt a strong urge to put his arm around her shoulders, but he resisted it. They were steadily becoming more intimate but he could wait a little longer for physical contact, hoping it would be welcome to her when it came. Instead, he said, "There's an art gallery I'd been intending to visit when I had to spend time with you at the hospital instead. It has just moved to new premises in a splendid old building and I want to see how it has been rearranged. Have you heard of the Courtauld Gallery?"

"No, I don't think I have. What kind of pictures do they have there?"

"They're best known for some wonderful French Impressionists; but the collection includes interesting early stuff as well. It's not very big, and so you can look around the lot without feeling exhausted at the end. I wondered if you'd like to come with me – maybe if you have some time off next weekend?"

"That's a super idea." She looked up at him with a sparkle of enthusiasm in her eyes, and again he wanted to hug her. But he refrained.

As they passed along the side of Brunswick Square, with the trees looming bare and skeletal through the darkness, he asked, "At which end of Judd Street is your building?"

"At this end – quite close now," she replied; and in a couple of minutes they were standing at the foot of a short flight of steps leading to the front door of a medium-sized mansion block of flats. Dorcas stood in front of him and looked up into his face.

"Thanks for a brilliant evening," she said. "I'll give you a bell about when I'm going to be free next weekend."

Then she placed a hand on each of his shoulders, stood on tiptoe, and kissed him swiftly and softly on his lips.

By the time he had recovered from his surprise she was at the top of the steps. "Goodnight. Sleep tight," he called after her.

Before closing the door behind her she turned around and gave him a final dazzling smile.

As he walked back down Judd Street with rain beginning to fall Dan experienced a strong desire to emulate Gene Kelly, and he even broke into the first few steps of a dance. But although the tune was in his head he couldn't remember the words – and he didn't have an umbrella.

* * *

On the following Monday morning Dan still retained a little of that Saturday night sense of elation. He felt certain that Dorcas wanted to move to a more intimate relationship and now he had before him the positive task of planning how to take her in that direction. It could only be enjoyable.

As he reached up for his winter raincoat the letter-box rattled and several items of post came through the front door. He stooped to pick them up and recognized a travel company brochure and what he guessed was an estate agent's offer to sell his flat for him. The third envelope was unfamiliar. The address was typed in unusually large letters, and on one corner was printed *From the Office of the Prime Minister*.

Bemused, he slit open the envelope with one finger and extracted the letter. Headed *10 Downing Street* in bold, black lettering, it informed him that he had been nominated for an OBE in the New Year Honours. Turning over the page, he read: 'Citation: (to be printed in the London Gazette) Chairman, World History Education Network. For services to the teaching of history.'

His first response was to ask himself whether he ought to accept the offer. On more than one occasion he had heard sneering references to the OBE as standing for 'Other Buggers' Efforts' and the CBE (which his father held, having earlier received an OBE for his part in the planning and execution of Operation Overlord) as 'Captured By the Establishment'. For every friend who would be pleased on his behalf there would be an acquaintance, or maybe even a colleague, who would sneer at his suspected vanity.

However, he decided that the award was just one more tool in life that could be used either well or badly. It would give pleasure to those who really were his friends, and at least one of them – he suspected Leo – must have had a hand in nominating him. The announcement would give a boost, albeit a tiny one, to public recognition of WHEN; and the letters after his name would even convey a small benefit to CPEEE, since few people would be aware that they were not connected with his work on its behalf. And the award should actually provide him with little temptation to thoughts of vainglory – it wasn't exactly a peerage, and it wouldn't be much use in securing a table at a fashionable restaurant, in the unlikely event of him ever wanting to book one.

So he decided to accept.

CHAPTER TEN 2 December 1989

Dorcas was still talking about the Courtauld Gallery pictures as they entered the Victoria Embankment Gardens by the gate at the Savoy Street end. Dan had been impressed by the enthusiasm with which she had greeted every new discovery in the gallery. He said, "At this time of year there's not much colour in these gardens but they do have some very interesting statues along the path. They're reminders of odd corners of history that a lot of people might have forgotten."

"I expect I never knew them," said Dorcas.

"Well, this first one is of somebody your background would probably help you to understand. He was very religious and also very radical in his politics, which is a combination that has quite often happened in Britain. His name is Sir Wilfred Lawson."

"He looks very stern and serious," said Dorcas.

"That's true, but oddly enough he had a reputation as a great humourist – inside the House of Commons. It could be that he didn't have much competition. In later years he was a founder of the temperance movement."

Pausing to look up at the formidable figure, Dorcas said, "That wasn't a bad thing to be. I used to think Mammy was silly when she told me that drink was invented by the devil, and when I went to Trinidad I had the odd glass of rum, though I didn't really like the taste. But when I saw how many people came into A and E because of booze – often other people's boozing – I thought she wasn't far wrong. It was easy for me to give it up again because I'd never really got into it."

"So that was why you didn't want to have wine at dinner last week?"

"Spot on. It saves me a lot of money, too."

"Well, after wine comes women and song," he said as they moved along the path. "The semi-naked lady on the monument over there is mourning for the great composer, Arthur Sullivan. Have you heard of him?"

"Yes, of course. There was a Gilbert and Sullivan Society in St Lucia that used to put on the operas. They were mostly white people, and one or two Indians. I can't remember the names of the shows because I wasn't allowed to go to them – the theatre was sinful – but I remember seeing the posters. He must have been very popular to have a monument like that."

"The next chap you can see on the other side was busy about a hundred years earlier and he did something that was very useful at the time, though you might not be so enthusiastic about what it turned into later on. He was the founder of Sunday schools."

She went across to the statue and read the name, "Robert Raikes – I've never heard of him. But I used to have to go to Sunday school every week and it was really boring. Mammy was one of the teachers – I think she still is."

"When Raikes started his schools the purpose was very different," said Dan. "He was concerned about all the kids who, in those days, had to work for six days a week and were never taught to read and write. That was why he organized schools on Sunday, and until the law provided for all children to go to school those schools made life better for a lot of people."

"So he really did deserve a statue," she said. Then, as they walked on, she exclaimed, "There's a little statue of a camel with a man on its back. Who's that in memory of?"

As they approached the small memorial Dan replied, "It's in memory of the men who served in the Camel Corps in the First World War. The Corps was formed to deal with the problem of moving quickly across desert areas in the Middle East. Your mother would probably be interested in this one, because they helped to drive the Turks out of Palestine and that was the beginning of the move to set up a national home for the Jews."

"Oh yes. I've listened to sermons about how Jesus is going to come back once the Jews have taken over the whole of Palestine and the Anti-Christ appears and starts attacking them. According to Pastor Mullen it's all predicted in the Book of Revelation. Even when I was a kid I thought that was a bit far-fetched."

"The man in the big statue farther back would have shared your reservations, I think," said Dan. "Have you heard of the Scottish poet, Robert Burns?"

"Of course I have. We learned some of his poems at school. I think it's good having to learn poetry by heart. One of them came back to me when... when things went wrong with Raj. Maybe you know it. It goes:

Had we never loved so kindly,
Had we never loved so blindly,

Dan completed the verse:

Never met and never parted
We had ne'er been broken-hearted.

"The teacher said it was an example of how deeply he felt emotion, but I'm not sure about that," said Dorcas. "From what I've read about him he moved on pretty quickly from one girl to another. I think he might just have been giving advice to guys that it wasn't a good idea to get too deeply involved with a girl. Maybe he'd once done that himself and didn't want to do it again."

"I'd never thought of that interpretation before," said Dan. "You might be right. He wasn't exactly a model of fidelity. And it could explain why he was such a mixture of passion and promiscuity.

"It's beginning to look as if we might have some rain; so I think we ought to take to the Tube. There's a station just through the end of the Gardens. Would you be willing to take a chance on my culinary skills and sample some home-made spaghetti this evening, or would you rather go to a restaurant again? I won't be offended if you opt for a professional cook."

To his great delight she put her hand on his arm and said, "Oh, I'd love to see where you live. But I'll tell you what I really think about your cooking; so don't expect any flattery."

"I know better than to expect flattery from you," he said, and gave her a quick hug around her shoulders.

Even though they had a change of trains at Piccadilly Circus the journey to Holborn took them only fifteen minutes, and it was not long before they were inside the flat and Dan was relieving her of her blue winter coat. Underneath it she wore a dark green sweater over a knee-length, Black Watch tartan skirt, which fitted so perfectly that he felt physically aroused the moment she turned her back to him. But he restrained himself and said, "The bathroom is on the right, if you want it."

"The flat is bigger than I thought it would be from the outside," she said. "How many rooms do you have?"

"Just bedroom, living-room and kitchen," he replied, "but they're all quite spacious, as you'll see. I usually eat in the kitchen, but I'd be happy to set up the table here, if you prefer," he added as he led her into the living-room.

"I'd like to eat in the kitchen if you'll let me help with the cooking," she replied.

When she had surveyed the living-room, remarking on how much she liked the nineteenth-century prints of London buildings that hung on the walls, they went through to the kitchen. Dan immediately turned on the electric oven, to heat it up for baking a Marks and Spencer ciabatta.

"This is nice," she said. "There's plenty of space for the table. I like round tables. You could fit five or six people around it, couldn't you?"

"It's not often I have to lay it even for two, although sometimes my mother looks in to check up on me. I think she still finds it a bit difficult to believe that I know how to look after myself."

"I think mothers can never really accept that their children have grown up – at least until they have grandchildren, I suppose," said Dorcas. "Nice washer-dryer you have. I wish I had one."

"Maybe you'll show me your kitchen one day," he said, and gave her another quick hug around her shoulders.

"You like touching, don't you?" she said, glancing up at him over her shoulder.

"I like touching *you*," he replied, taking a step backward. "Am I out of order?"

She laughed and shook her head. "Of course you're not. I like being touched – by you. You've been holding back, haven't you?"

He felt an urgent surge of desire. "Not any more. If I had eight hands they'd be all over your beautiful body."

"I once saw an old film on TV called *Dear Octopus*. Maybe that's what I ought to call you," she said.

He chuckled. "I have actually been called that – a long time ago," he said; and the memory of Catherine on a beach in St Lucia flashed into his mind as his right hand moved swiftly down to Dorcas' bottom. And then a more recent memory inspired him to say, "I think it's time I checked out what you told me about being a different colour from the waist down."

"Are you doubting my word?" she asked, as she put her arms around his neck.

"Not in the least, but I'd just like to see this wonder of nature for myself. You've had several chances to look at me without my clothes on. Could it be my turn now?"

To his delight she replied, "OK", and added with characteristic practicality, "But maybe the kitchen isn't the best place to take off our clothes."

"Quite right," he said, and putting one arm around her waist and the other across the back of her thighs, he lifted her into the air. "I'll carry you through to the bedroom, because it's a very special occasion."

She seemed to be totally relaxed in his arms, and giggled as he bore her through the living-room to the bedroom door. "Now I know what it really means to be 'swept off your feet'," she said.

"I wouldn't want you to be doing a striptease for me," he said as he set her down. "Will you allow me to… help you reveal the truth – using all my eight arms?"

He was permitted to unzip her skirt while she removed her sweater, revealing that her firm little breasts needed no brassiere – and that her nipples were already erect. The waistband of her lacy white knickers and her black suspender belt were too low to conceal the surprisingly clear division of colour at the level of her waist: dark brown below and light brown above. In awe he knelt down in front of her and planted a gentle kiss on her belly button.

It was not many minutes before she had unbuckled his belt while with eager fingers he undid the buttons of his shirt. Content now that her objective was identical with his own, he employed his lips in kissing rather than talking until their preparations were complete. When he produced a packet of condoms she laughed and said, "That saves me from having to send you to fetch my handbag."

* * *

It was more than half-an-hour before they reached a pause in their strenuous activity and lay perspiring side by side on top of the duvet.

"I knew you were going to be good," said Dorcas. "From the way you talked I could see you understood how to treat a girl, and from the way you looked at me I could see how much you wanted it." She turned her head and kissed him on the cheek. He was about to say, 'Maybe I was good because you were so good' but he checked himself. Her previous experience in bed was none of his business.

"How much I wanted *you*," he said instead, raising himself on one elbow to look down at her. "And the more I have the more I will want; but I think we ought to renew our strength now by having something to eat. It's a good job I hadn't put the ciabatta into the oven or it would be burnt to a crisp by now."

Dignity was not an issue as they ate their spaghetti sitting at the kitchen table, Dan in his shirt and boxer shorts and Dorcas clad in his winter dressing-gown with the sleeves rolled up.

"When can you next get some time off from work?" he asked, as he mopped up the last of the tomato and basil sauce with a slice of ciabatta.

"I'll be free again next Saturday, after lunchtime."

"Would you like to come with me to *A Midsummer Night's Dream* at the Barbican Theatre? I've heard it's a very good production; and the part of Bottom is played by an actor called David Troughton I found myself sitting next to at a cricket match last summer. The reviewers have said he's very good in the part. We could go to the matinee and afterwards come back here for a little something."

"I'd love to do that," she said, and wiped her lips on one of the napkins he'd found at the bottom of a drawer. "But let's have something that doesn't take too long to cook. Then we might have time for... for... a big something afterwards. Like tonight, I won't be able to stay late because I'll be on the ward early next morning."

"I think you can read my mind," he said.

"That's not very difficult," she replied. "Just like mine, it's a bit one-track at the moment."

He laughed exultantly. "It would be great if we could have a longer time together. Will they be giving you any time off at Christmas?"

"I've volunteered to work on Christmas Eve and Boxing Day, but I'll have Christmas Day off."

"Would you like to spend it here with me?"

"I can't think of anything I'd like more." She came around the table to stand beside him, and kissed the top of his head.

"I think we might find one or two interesting games to play, like people do at Christmas," he said, slipping his hand inside the dressing-gown and feeling once again the electrifyingly silken smoothness of her hip.

"The kind of games that involve taking your clothes off?" she asked.

"You've guessed it in one," he replied, patting her bottom.

CHAPTER ELEVEN 17 December, 1989

In the years after Dan and Vera had finally left home it had become a tradition for Arthur and Margarita to host a Sunday lunch for their circle of oldest friends a week before Christmas. Ruth and Daniel, Nancy, Rebecca and Roddy were the usual guests, but this year Dan had also been invited. He suspected that his mother was still concerned about his wellbeing because of the spell in hospital with psoriasis, and he resolved to make an opportunity to reassure her by indicating that there had been a revival in his love life.

The menu was always the same. It began with a vegetable soup, in deference to Nancy's vegetarian principles, and then there was fish pie (Nancy's diet didn't exclude fish), and in conclusion a Yorkshire-style apple pie with custard. During the first two courses conversation was muted while they all concentrated on enjoying the results of Margarita's culinary skills which, as she always reminded them, owed everything to time spent with Arthur's mother in York and nothing to her upbringing in Spain.

As the plates of apple pie were being passed around Arthur remarked that in a fortnight it would be the fiftieth anniversary of the day when he reported for his Army training. "And I suppose you would have been just finishing yours, Daniel," he added.

"No, I still had a month to do at Sandhurst after Christmas," said Daniel. "We were into the Phoney War by then, and there didn't seem to be much sense of urgency. I even had a week's leave at Christmas that enabled me to pop over to Northern Ireland to see my family. I didn't see them again for five and a half years."

"I seem to remember that food rationing didn't start until after Christmas," said Ruth.

"Last week I met an old friend who hasn't seen his family for fifty years, but he's hoping in the New Year to be able at last to visit the ones who are still alive," said Daniel. "I was very touched when he said he felt great gratitude to me and all the colleagues I'd worked with who had made

NATO a reality. It was the reason why his country was going to be free at last."

"Is that your Polish friend, Andy?" Arthur asked.

"Yes. I get together with him about twice every year. It's ironic that we went to war fifty years ago to defend the freedom of the Poles from the Nazis and it's only this year that they've finally regained it – from the Communists."

"Did you first meet your friend during the War?" Dan asked.

"He was a liaison officer with the Polish Second Corps when I was at Alexander's HQ. He actually went back to Italy for the funeral when his old commander, General Anders, was buried at Monte Cassino in 1970. The general wanted to be buried alongside his men who were killed in that dreadful battle. They were the bravest of the brave."

Dan remembered that his 'uncle' had himself been at Monte Cassino and could be considered a reliable judge of bravery. For a few minutes there was silence around the table as the apple pie was consumed. Then his mother said, "Yesterday we went to see *A Midsummer Night's Dream* at the Barbican. I thought it was a very good performance. Has anyone else seen it?"

Dan seized the moment of opportunity. "Yes, I took… a friend to see it last week. We thought it was brilliant. She was really tickled by David Troughton's performance as Bottom."

His mother was quick to respond. "Was this a… particular friend?" she asked, with an expectant smile.

"Maybe. I haven't known her very long. She was one of the nurses who looked after me so brilliantly at the hospital. Her name is Dorcas."

"A very Biblical name," Daniel commented.

"She says her mother is very religious. She was born in St Lucia, where I once spent some time, of course, but she would only have been a schoolgirl then."

"If she works in a hospital you'd better be careful, with this flu epidemic that's going around," said Nancy.

"I'll be sure to tell her to wash her hands," said Dan, grinning.

"So she's West Indian. Is she black?" Ruth asked, a little tentatively.

"Actually she is a unique combination of Chinese, Indian, Afro and European, and by anyone's standards the outcome is incredibly beautiful. You probably think I'm biased, but I'd be surprised if anyone could disagree. The whole ward used to brighten up when she came into it."

"When are we going to meet her? I hope you'll soon be able to bring her here, so we can judge for ourselves," said his mother.

"That might be a bit premature. I'm only just getting to know her. But if she'd like to come I might bring her to see you in the New Year." He decided it was time to change the subject and went on, "Has anyone seen the new exhibition at the National Gallery, the one on 'Art in the Making'?"

"I've been meaning to go but I haven't got around to it yet," said Ruth. "Would you like to come with me one day this week, Rebecca? The Gallery is usually quite quiet just before Christmas."

"That's a great idea. Can we look in our diaries before we go home?" Rebecca replied. Dan knew that they often went to art exhibitions together, and when he was a schoolboy they had sometimes taken him with them, giving him the introduction to his lifelong interest in paintings.

"We'll have coffee in the sitting-room," said Margarita, "and nobody is to offer to help with the dishes. I'll have plenty of time for that when you've all gone home."

"And that's my cue to put the kettle on," said Arthur, getting up from the table and heading for the kitchen.

Dan recognized one of the little rituals that had grown up since his parents had moved from his boyhood suburban home into their Marylebone mansion flat. In his childhood the rituals had been different, but there had even then usually been a pre-Christmas meal with old friends.

As they settled into comfortable chairs in the sitting-room Roddy asked, "Has anybody been to a carol concert?"

"We're going to one this evening," said Margarita, entering the room with a tray of cups and saucers. "Arthur's Mam always used to sing in a carol concert and he likes to keep up the connection. We're going to hear the Bach Choir at the Albert Hall."

"I'm going to a concert at the Queen Elizabeth Hall on Thursday," said Nancy. "It's being conducted by Donald Cashmore, who used to be the organist at Kingsway Hall when I went to church there. Leo's going to come with me and then take me back to Newingham Magna on Friday, to spend Christmas with the family."

"I noticed that Leo took part in that debate they had in the Lords on the creative industries," said Arthur. "He was in favour of computer studies being in the curriculum, if I remember rightly."

"I think that might be partly because young Freddie has been very enthusiastic. He wants to study computer science at university, if that's possible," said Nancy.

"How long is it since you last saw the grandchildren?" asked Rebecca.

"They came up to town at half-term; so it wasn't very long ago. We went to the British Museum together. Virginia was very keen to see the Sutton Hoo treasure, but I think at the moment Freddie is more interested in what he can find on the small screen."

"Teenage obsessions can be quite intense," said Ruth, "but if it leads on to something he can take up professionally that might be very good."

Arthur arrived with the coffee-pot and began to pour out. "It's a brand called 'Old Brown Java'," he said. "We really like it."

"Have you seen any of the broadcasts from the Commons since they let the cameras in?" Roddy asked Arthur.

"Yes, I have. I'm not sure that television is going to do anything positive for the reputation of the House. Even in my day there were times when I was glad to notice that the Public Gallery was pretty empty. But politics has started to be more interesting in the past few weeks, since Anthony Meyer made his challenge to Mrs Thatcher. He was never going to win, of course. A split in the Tory Party is the only thing at the moment that's likely to open the door to an election victory for Labour."

"But aren't Labour already well ahead in the opinion polls?" said Nancy.

"They are; but there's a recession looming up and Labour still hasn't got a credible economic policy," Arthur replied. "When it comes to a vote a lot of people are going to stay with the devil they know."

Dan decided that he wanted to pay a visit to the bathroom and slipped out of the room while the coffee-cups were being collected. On the way back his eye was caught by a photograph hanging in the corridor. It showed his father and mother standing outside Buckingham Palace on the day that Arthur was 'advanced' to CBE. He was reminded that he hadn't yet decided when to tell them about his own forthcoming OBE. Today, with other people around would not be appropriate, he thought, affirming his belief that the traditional rule of privacy ought to be maintained, with exception being made only for the people closest to oneself. He would tell them on Christmas Eve; and on Christmas Day he would tell Dorcas. His PA, Anne, also deserved to know, and he would tell her when the office closed for the Christmas break.

Back in the sitting-room everyone was laughing as Roddy described an incident that happened when he was playing his first West End part, as a – non-speaking – Covent Garden porter in *Pygmalion* at the Haymarket. He had been carrying a stack of baskets on his head, in the traditional manner when he'd stumbled and the baskets had cascaded across the stage, "Margaret Rutherford was playing Eliza," said Roddy. "She did an instant ad lib: 'Oo's a clumsy boy, then?' and the audience roared with laughter. It actually got the performance off to a very relaxed start."

"Did that happen on a night before we went to see you performing or after?" Ruth asked.

"I think it must have been after, because I seem to remember you came soon after the play opened. Daniel had just joined the Territorials and he thought he might be caught up in extra training sessions. Wasn't it just about the time that Hitler signed his 'Pact of Steel' with Mussolini?"

"It was," said Ruth. "I think we were starting to realize then that we'd begun to slide down a short slope to disaster. I remember it was about the time my headmistress had just visited the school in Berkshire where the girls were all going to be evacuated if war broke out. We didn't have long to wait."

"Now we've just been told officially that the Cold War is over, I hope we can start to believe that our grandchildren will never have to go through an experience like that one," said Margarita.

"I hope so, too, but I wouldn't put money on it," said Daniel. "The Cold War has left the world littered with millions of nasty weapons from Kalashnikovs to nuclear bombs, and there are still plenty of nutters around who'd be only too willing to use them. If the international community can only get its act together there should be no more big catastrophes, but we've still to see that happening. However, I mustn't go banging on about my pet obsession. 'Tis the season to be jolly, and we have more good reasons for being jolly than we've had at any Christmas I can remember."

"For some reason that reminds me of the play we saw at the Young Vic last week," said Rebecca. "It was an adaptation of Dickens' *Christmas Carol*. There was a very funny incident right at the end, when Scrooge reveals that he has been converted to benevolence and tells Bob Crachit that he's going to raise his salary. A little boy, about ten I should think, was sitting in front of us with his parents and he said, in a loud, clear voice, 'Raise his celery? Why would he do that?'"

When the laughter had subsided Ruth asked Dan, "Have you any plans for Christmas Day? I hope you're not going to be sitting on your own, eating baked beans and watching television."

"Thank you, but you don't need to worry about that," he replied. "My plans don't involve television – apart from the Queen's Christmas Message – nor baked beans either, and with a bit of luck it might be the best Christmas I've had for a long time.

CHAPTER TWELVE Christmas Day, 1989

Dorcas had surprised Dan by asking if they could go to church on Christmas morning. It would make her mother happy when she next wrote to her, she explained. So, when she had deposited her little suitcase at his flat they walked together through the deserted streets to Bloomsbury Baptist Church, where Dan discovered that he remembered most of the carols from his schooldays. Afterwards, as they returned along Bloomsbury Way and Theobalds Road, there were still very few people around.

"Christmas Day is the only day in the year when the centre of London is virtually empty," Dan remarked. "The shops are all closed and there is no public transport. I pity any foreign tourists who have made the mistake of being here."

"Hospital isn't a good place to be, either," said Dorcas. "No doctors around, and less than half the nurses. Yesterday we did our best to cheer up the patients that were left, but it's pretty hard going. If you're feeling really bad you might not want to be cheered up. I was on the men's surgical ward."

"They would have had to be in a really bad way not to be cheered up by having you around," said Dan.

When they arrived home he announced, "The turkey has been in the oven on a slow roast and it should be ready at about half past one – if my Katie Stewart Cookbook is correct, and she's never wrong. So I just have to do the vegetables, and they're all ready to go. I thought you'd like to have a traditional English Christmas dinner – although I suppose there's been a lot of that at the hospital."

"It will be nice to see how it tastes when it's been done properly," she said. "Can I help with the cooking? Maybe you have an apron I could wear?"

"I think there's one at the bottom of the drawer with the tablecloths and things," he replied, opening the drawer and beginning to rummage. Right at the bottom he found an apron decorated with pictures of penguins. It had belonged to Catherine, though he couldn't remember her wearing it.

Dorcas was dressed in a crimson-coloured knitted wool frock that clung to her contours as if she had been sewn into it. When he had tied the apron strings behind her waist Dan could not resist the temptation to take that perfect posterior into the palms of his hands.

"If you can't keep your hands to yourself until we've had dessert this dinner's never going to get on to the table," she said, twisting her head to look up at him.

"As usual, you're absolutely right," he replied, giving her a swift pat and a light kiss on her lips before releasing her. "Now it's time to tackle the Brussels sprouts."

"What's in the big saucepan that you've just turned on?" she enquired.

"That's the Christmas pudding, having its final half-hour. It's already been boiled for about three hours. But I must confess I didn't make it. Every year my mother makes three puddings; one for herself and Dad and any guests; one for me; and one to take to my sister, Vera, where they'll be spending today. She had the recipe from my grandmother, who copied it from the *Radio Times* during the War. It was devised by a famous cookery writer called Marguerite Patten, and although it's an 'austerity' recipe everyone that's tasted it seems to agree that it's one of the best. I'm afraid I haven't done a Saint Clement's Sauce to accompany it, but I did remember to get some double cream from Marks and Spencer."

* * *

When the pudding was finally served Dorcas agreed that, although it would not be good for her waistline, it was delicious. As he poured the coffee Dan remarked, "It's a variety called 'Old Brown Java'. My father recommended it. He's an expert on coffee – or thinks he is."

She sipped the coffee and said, "I like it. It's strong without being bitter. In the Caribbean people reckon that Jamaican 'Blue Mountain' is the best."

Coffee drunk, they cleared the dishes, and Dan insisted they should leave them in the sink while they watched the Queen's Christmas Message. Sitting side by side on the small sofa that he called a 'snuggler' they turned on the television.

When a picture of the Albert Hall packed with children appeared on the screen Dan commented, "This is a turn-up for the book. She usually does the broadcast from home." And immediately the Queen confirmed his remark, saying:

I usually make my Christmas Broadcast to the Commonwealth form Windsor or Buckingham Palace. This year I thought I would use the presence of two thousand children at this occasion organized by Save the Children Fund in the Albert Hall, here in the heart of London, to send this special message to the children of the Commonwealth.

"SCF are lucky to have Princess Anne as their president. I'm sure it was she who thought up this wheeze," said Dan.

"Shush!" said Dorcas; and they listened in silence as the Queen went on to talk about the threats facing the world, from the 'greenhouse effect', pollution and deforestation. The future of life on earth, she said, depended on how we behaved towards one another, and how we treated the plants and the animals. When she then briefly recounted the parable of the Good Samaritan and said that it wasn't difficult to apply that story to our own times Dorcas remarked, "Mammy will love this bit."

In her concluding sentences the Queen ventured to hope that, because of the recent changes in Eastern Europe, the Nineties might become a time of peace and tranquillity, when people would work together for the benefit of the planet as a whole. And she ended:

In the hope that we will be kind and loving to one another, not just on Christmas Day but throughout the year, I wish you all a very happy Christmas. God bless you.

Pressing the remote control to switch off, Dan said, "I think it's time we obeyed her royal command – don't you?"

"Which command do you mean?"

"To be kind and loving to one another," he replied, standing up and then reaching down to pick her up in his arms. She giggled and kissed him repeatedly on the cheek as he carried her to the bedroom.

"I can't understand how Carlos can keep it up for so long without having a climax. I must have come about eight times already and he shows no sign of giving himself a break," said Dorcas, as they returned for the third time to the missionary position.

"I've never quite understood that myself," said Dan. "When he and I were both beginners it was difficult getting him to hold back. I think maybe it was finding out how much he was enjoying himself that made him want to keep going for as long as he could. Of course, I could pretend that he's really very altruistic and just wants to go on giving you pleasure for as long as he possibly can, but I think his programming might be a bit more primeval than that."

Dorcas emitted a small moan of satisfaction. "I don't mind how long he stays in," she said. "I must be pretty primeval myself."

"I wonder how it would be if he just stayed still inside for a while. Would you enjoy that too?" he asked.

"Will he stay up if you don't move him?"

"I don't know. Let's give it a try." He lay quite still, luxuriating in the softness of flesh on flesh all the way from his chest to his ankles, and especially in the sensation of being held inside her body. Then suddenly he felt her internal muscles begin to contract and expand spasmodically, and although he exerted all his strength to stay inside, within a couple of minutes Carlos was expelled like the cork from a champagne bottle – only without any audible 'pop'. Looking at each other in mutual bewilderment, they spontaneously burst into laughter.

"I never knew that was possible," he said. "I was trying my hardest to stay inside."

"I really couldn't help it," said Dorcas. "I've never known anything like it. I suppose my muscles must have got the idea that Carlos was a baby, and they were programmed to push him out. But they never told us anything about that kind of possibility in midwifery classes. Let me give him a kiss and tell him I'm sorry."

It was not very long before normal service was resumed.

* * *

After another hour of leisurely lovemaking they both agreed it was time for an intermission. "I'll put the kettle on," said Dan. "We could be doing with a cuppa. If you like, you can wear my winter dressing-gown. You'll need to roll up the sleeves, but I think the hem will stay clear of the floor on you."

He took his black and red woollen dressing-gown from the wardrobe and tossed it to her; and then he covered his own nakedness with his navy blue padded winter raincoat.

"While I'm making tea and warming up some mince pies you might like to watch the news on the telly," he said. "I think it's on BBC 1 just about now. For some reason nothing that's newsworthy is supposed to happen on Christmas Day; so I suppose it will be all those worthy messages from the Pope and the Archbishop of Canterbury and the Queen, and how everybody's having a jolly time."

"Well, *we* certainly are," said Dorcas, descending from the bed and wrapping herself in his dressing-gown. "I bet a lot of people who've been doing all the things they're supposed to do on Christmas Day would be envious if they knew how we've been spending our time."

As he was loading the tray with mugs, plates and swiftly microwaved Marks and Spencer 'luxury' mince pies he heard the television come on in the living-room. When he carried the tray through Dorcas exclaimed, "You were wrong about the news. The Romanians have just executed their president and his wife. They were tried by a military court and then shot immediately afterwards."

He set down the tray on the dining-table and heard Jill Dando begin to talk about the Queen's Christmas Message. Dorcas switched off the television and came to the table. "Wasn't it only a day or two ago they were out in the streets rioting in Romania?" she asked. "Was the president – I can never remember his name – really very bad?"

"Ceausescu – he was certainly a nasty piece of work. Strangely, there was a time in the Seventies when everybody thought he was going to be a liberalizer. He'd dissented when the Russians intervened in Czechoslovakia, and he started mixing nationalism with his communism. Even the poor old Queen was obliged to entertain him and his equally nasty wife when they came here on an official visit. But it wasn't long before he was providing another example of the way that 'people's republics' seem to be carefully designed to ensure that it's only a very small number of people who actually own the republic."

"That's like what happened in Grenada a few years ago, when the small number tried to become even smaller," said Dorcas. "I had a cousin who went to work there, but he got out after the first coup – the Bishop one. If the Americans hadn't gone in after the second coup, when Bishop was killed, it would be a really nasty place by now. My cousin, George, has gone back there and he says he likes it. The people are very friendly, in spite of what they went through when the communists were in charge."

"Talking of the Caribbean," said Dan, "I notice that later this evening the BBC is screening one of Agatha Christie's Miss Marple stories, called *A Caribbean Mystery*. Would you like to watch it while we're having another 'intermission', before we finally go to bed for the night? You could tell me if the background is really authentic. We can pretend we're sitting in the back row of the cinema and misbehave ourselves like teenagers."

"I wasn't allowed to go to the cinema when I was a teenager. It was sinful," said Dorcas, taking a sip from her mug of tea. "I heard all about it from my mates at school and I was very envious. Have you got any popcorn?"

"Afraid I haven't; but there's a box of Lindt chocolates. They're the very best."

"Then they'll be just about good enough for me," She helped herself to a mince pie. "Mince pies are another of your Christmas rituals, aren't they? We've had a lot of them at the hospital this year."

"And I expect you'll be having some more tomorrow. They usually last until Boxing Day, or longer. I suppose you'll have to leave at the crack of dawn to start your shift."

"Yes. I hope you have an alarm clock."

"Don't worry. I'll set it at whatever time you tell me to. And I'll be taking you to the hospital in a taxi. It can stop around the corner if you want it to. But we'll need to be strong-minded about going to sleep tonight early enough for you to have a proper rest."

"That might not be so easy," she said, finishing the mince pie and snuggling up against him. "It's been a long time since I was able to spend the whole night with somebody... somebody I really wanted to be with."

"I hope it'll never be as long again," he said; and then he realized there was something he ought to do, but not just yet.

CHAPTER THIRTEEN 12 January 1990

When Anne came in with the morning post she announced, "I'm afraid we still have a problem with the judges. Lord Callaghan isn't going to be available to chair, after all. So it's back to the drawing-board."

"That's a nuisance," said Dan. "His name would have carried a lot of weight. I wonder if we might be able to persuade Dr Patel, the Director of LSE. I think my father might still have some contact there. I'll have a word with him at the weekend."

"Well, you should have plenty of time. There won't be much on the television to distract you – though I think there's a new *Antiques Roadshow* series starting on Sunday. That's always interesting."

"Did you watch the final part of *Oranges aren't the only fruit*?" Dan asked. "I thought it was a good adaptation. Some books don't work well on television."

"I videoed it but we haven't watched it yet. It's all about a girl growing up in a fundamentalist family, isn't it?"

"That's right. I was particularly interested because I have a friend who had that kind of upbringing, although I think her mother wasn't so aggressively pious as Jeanette Winterson's. I suspect that kind of absolutist religious upbringing often produces the opposite effect to the one intended by the parents, once the kids are able to discover for themselves the realities of the wider world."

"I'm glad to say I didn't have that experience," said Anne, sorting out the letters on his desk. "You'll see that we've had another application in the 'Long-term Commitment' category. It's from the Unilever Plantations division."

"That's interesting. I met the chap who chairs that department when we had the seminar on sustainable development last year – name of Davidson, I think. He's had a remarkable career. The Malaysians made him a 'Datuk', the equivalent of a knight, for solving a problem with pollinating their oil palms. It's added several hundred million pounds a year to the country's earnings, he told me."

"If he's still in charge there you'll probably meet him again," said Anne. "We now have three good applications in that category. But we've only had two for 'Encouraging Local Initiatives'."

"I suppose you could say that shows how important it is that we're making companies more aware of it. I don't think I have any engagements today – do I?"

"No, there's nothing in the diary. But John has asked if he can have some time with you. He's thought of an idea for a project involving Business Studies students."

"Sounds interesting. Does he have any thoughts about funding for the project?"

"No, but I do."

"Great – then I'd like you to join in the discussion. Ask John if eleven o'clock would suit him. If it does I'll make us some coffee to stimulate the thought processes."

* * *

The day proved to be a productive one, and Dan decided to leave the office half-an-hour early, to give himself more time to prepare dinner. To save time he took the shortest route home, striding along Clerkenwell Road, rather than the 'scenic route' which he usually favoured because it included a detour through Gray's Inn Gardens. Dorcas was coming to dinner and by having the food ready to go on the table when she arrived he would maximise the time available for being close to her.

They hadn't been able to see each other since Christmas because of the flu epidemic. Dorcas had had to work extra shifts to cover for colleagues who were ill, and had needed what free time was left to catch up on her sleep. They had had to cancel a planned visit to an exhibition of pictures by Frans Hals at the Royal Academy – which would, of course, have been followed up by a return to the flat, and an opportunity to ask the question that was now uppermost in Dan's mind.

102

On Christmas night as he lay in bed looking at the beauty of her sleeping face he had resolved that he must not allow their relationship to become one in which he could be accused of 'using' her for his own pleasure – even though it was pretty clear that she was having lots of pleasure, too. And he was also conscious that there must be a lot of other men around who would be only too happy to be in his position – young doctors at the hospital, for a start. It was time to leave her in no doubt that what he wanted was a permanent relationship – or, as he expected her mother would put it, he wanted to 'make an honest woman of her'.

As he crossed the street towards the Holborn Library he reflected that Dorcas deserved a more spacious home than his little flat, comfortable though it might be for a single occupant. Once the date of the wedding had been agreed he would talk to her about where she would like to live. A mansion flat like his parents', and in the Marylebone area where they lived, not too far from the Regent's Park, might be an attractive proposition. At the moment his parents were both sprightly septuagenarians, but sooner or later one or both of them would begin to slow down, and then it could be helpful if he was living in their neighbourhood. But he would first have to hear what Dorcas thought about the idea.

The moment he arrived home he switched on the oven and took the shepherd's pie he had prepared the night before out of the fridge, along with a packet of peas that could be cooked in the microwave – a new-fangled device that his mother had persuaded him to install two years earlier. While the oven was heating up he laid the table in the kitchen, and then removed the Marks and Spencer *tarte au citron* slices from the fridge. No time was going to be lost on dinner; and the washing-up could wait till Saturday morning.

Dorcas arrived at exactly the time she had predicted, and when fond embraces had been exchanged they sat down to eat.

When they had come together for the third time, with Dorcas triumphantly on top of him, they admitted to being just a little exhausted, and were content to lie side by side on the bed. This was the moment when

103

he must ask the question, Dan decided. He raised himself on one elbow and looked down into her smiling face.

"Dorcas, I don't think I need to tell you how much happiness you've given me in these last few weeks. And I get the feeling you've enjoyed being with me, too. It's made me realize that I don't ever want this to come to an end. We fit together perfectly in so many ways – not just the one we've been demonstrating. And there are so many things I want to give you – not just tangible things, but all the love that you bring out in me. I want us to be really together from now on. Will you marry me, Dorcas?"

Her eyes opened wide in astonishment, and then she pushed herself up into a sitting position. "Oh, Dan, I wasn't expecting that," she said. "It's the first time I've ever been asked that question. I don't know what to say. You're the nicest person I know. If I was going to marry somebody I couldn't find anybody who was better. But I couldn't marry you. It's my Mammy – she'd be so unhappy. It would really hurt her… if I got married to somebody who was divorced. She believes that once you get married it's forever, and if you get divorced and do it again you're living in sin, and God will send both of you to hell. She really believes that, and I couldn't do it to her, after all that she has done for me."

"But what about what we've just been up to? What would she think about that?" he asked, pushing himself up to sit beside her.

"She doesn't know about it. That's the important thing. It doesn't bother her because I wouldn't tell her about it. But getting married is different. It's all about families, and you can't have secrets about it. I wouldn't want to, anyhow. And I don't think I really want to get married – but if I did it would be to somebody like you. Oh, you've made me so happy and now I've made you unhappy. I'm sorry."

Tears began to trickle down her cheeks and she shivered. Dan reached for the discarded duvet and pulled it up on to the bed, wrapping it around her.

"Don't cry," he said. "I just wanted to make things permanent for your sake – for both our sakes. But we don't have to get married if you don't want to. We can still have a permanent relationship."

"But we can't," she said, looking up at him with saddened eyes. "I was going to tell you before I went home tonight. At Christmas Mammy had a fall and broke her hip. It happened when she was putting up the decorations. Matthew wrote to me but the letter took longer to arrive because of Christmas. She's going to have an operation and then she'll have to take it easy for about six months. And then – it was a brilliant coincidence – I saw an advert in last week's *Nursing Times* for a Sister at the Victoria in St Lucia. I might not get the job, of course, but I think I have a pretty good chance. And I'd really like to be around to keep an eye on her till she gets back to normal again, if she ever does."

"So how soon would you be leaving?" he asked, feeling shocked by the speed at which his expectations were disintegrating.

"If I get the job it could be as soon as the end of February, because of a reorganization they're having at the hospital. I'm sorry it's so sudden, but I really was going to tell you tonight. I never thought it would all… get mixed up with something else."

She began to cry again and he held her to him closely, saying, "Don't be unhappy. You have to do what you think is right."

But he himself was very unhappy.

CHAPTER FOURTEEN 28 February, 1990

It was already getting dark when Dan emerged from Baker Street Station on his way to have dinner with Ruth and Daniel. They lived in a mews house only a few hundred yards away from his parents' mansion flat; and as he crossed the ever-busy Marylebone Road he remembered visiting them as a schoolboy in their first home, a flat in High Holborn. He used to persuade Daniel to show him military memorabilia from Italy and Korea; and he heard from Ruth so many stories about places they had visited that it fuelled his desire to travel and see the wider world for himself. Now Ruth had said, when inviting him to dinner, that they wanted to offer him a suggestion for a project related to WHEN.

She had, he reflected, always seemed to know instinctively when he was feeling low and in need of a boost to his morale. And he had rarely felt lower than he did at the moment, having finally said farewell to Dorcas. On Tuesday she had left for the Caribbean, and when he had offered to see her off at Heathrow she had declined, saying it would only make both of them sadder than they already were.

The streets were busy with people hurrying home at the end of the working week. As he turned into Upper Montagu Street he looked across to the block in which his parents lived and saw that the light was on in their living room. If it wasn't too late in the evening he would look in and have a quick word with them on his way home. Somehow he felt reassured because they were living so close to their oldest friends. Perhaps it was a selfish feeling, he reflected, because it relieved him of the need to keep more constantly in touch with them, now that they were entering the second half of their seventies – not that they seemed yet to be in any special need of his care and attention.

On arrival he was, as ever, greeted warmly, and taken into the sitting-room. Ruth said the casserole would be ready in about half-an-hour. (He knew she was not a cookery enthusiast, but she always produced simple dishes that he enjoyed.)

"Last week we were reflecting that, for the first time in years, neither of us is working on a book," said Daniel. "And then this idea emerged – I'm not sure who thought of it first – that we could collaborate on something that might actually be appropriate to publish under the aegis of WHEN. Of course, that would depend on whether your colleagues liked the idea. But we thought it would be best to talk to you about it first."

"I expect that hearing about your award may have subconsciously nudged the idea into existence," said Ruth.

"I'm all ears," said Dan. "Please tell me about it."

With a nod from Ruth, Daniel started to explain. "With the new millennium coming up at the end of this decade, we're thinking about a book that could look at significant trends in the history of Europe over the two AD millennia, through some of the visual evidence that still remains. The book would take the form of a travellers' handbook to significant cities, with each city being particularly representative of a century or period. The easiest example would be Rome, for taking a look at the decline and fall of the Roman Empire."

Ruth interjected, "We thought the title might be something like *A Time Travellers' Guide to Two Millennia in Europe*. And, of course, each chapter would have a second section on the city's visual evidence from other periods of history, with reference back to the main chapter on that period – maybe with some kind of colour-coding. In the Rome chapter, for example, there would be important entries on the Renaissance and on the rise of nationalism in the nineteenth century."

Daniel continued, "The aim would be to make the book a readable stimulant to getting interested in the way that Europe has developed over two thousand years, and at the same time a guide that travellers could use when visiting a particular city. Having some simple street maps would be important."

"Some well-chosen photos would also be useful," said Ruth, "but I'm not sure about the economics of that. We wouldn't want the book to be too expensive, especially if it was something WHEN was going to be associated with, and recommend to teachers."

"It's a fascinating idea," said Dan. "I think it could be a very useful addition to WHEN's repertoire. A book by two authors who are well established in two different genres could really widen the constituency. But I'll need to have a word with Sara and get her on board. I think she'll be enthusiastic – especially as you two would be doing most of the hard work."

"We've made some rough notes about possible chapters and links between them," said Ruth, picking up a folder from the coffee table. "You can have a look at them with Daniel while I see how the dinner is coming along."

* * *

When they had finished eating and were sipping their decaffeinated coffee Dan remarked, "Things really seem to be moving ahead in South Africa since Mandela was released. It was only about a fortnight ago and yet they're already talking about having negotiations between the ANC and the government."

"I never thought I'd see a peaceful solution to apartheid in my lifetime," said Daniel, "but with any luck it might just happen."

Dan nodded. "Given what's been happening in Russia, anything seems to be possible now – and I'm sure there's a connection with what's happening in South Africa that the historians will spell out one day," he said. "Incidentally, did you see that report last week – it wasn't given much prominence – about the death in Moscow of a British man who'd been a Communist spy in the diplomatic service, and who was supposed to have died in a road accident in Mexico about forty years ago? I wondered if you might even have come across him, because the report said he was in the Washington Embassy at that time, and I thought it must have been when you were working at the UN."

"We did, indeed, know Cyril Hamberly. He helped us move into our apartment when we went to Washington," said Ruth. "And then he became a bit too friendly, trying to find out from Daniel about the work he was doing."

"It was I who blew the whistle on him," said Daniel, "although it was only a vague suspicion based on some remarks he made when he was drunk. It was long before the Burgess and Maclean scandal, but at the time there was some anxiety about security because of information a defecting Soviet

108

official had given to the Canadians. Anyhow, I passed on my doubt to an old wartime pal called Ted Frobisher who was working in MI6. The final upshot was that the FBI watched Hamberly and spotted him making contact with a Russian. He was going to be pulled in once the diplomatic niceties had been sorted out between the Foreign Office and the Yanks, but somebody tipped him off and he did a runner. For reasons best known to itself the Foreign Office decided to have a cover-up, and it was announced that he'd gone on holiday to Mexico and had been killed in a car accident. Since he was known to be a heavy drinker the story sounded plausible, and after that he ceased to exist."

"Who do you think tipped him off?" Dan asked.

"Almost certainly it must have been Philby. I remember that my friend Ted told me at the time when the Yanks wanted to move in on him that there was only one person in counter-intelligence he could trust with the information because he was somebody who'd been pro-fascist before the War, and his name was Philby. That must have been about three years before Burgess and Maclean made a run for it."

"Was this chap Hamberly another product of Cambridge University?"

"No. He was actually at Oxford; and that makes me wonder whether there might not have been an Oxford 'ring' that has never been uncovered. I remember meeting Ted about ten years ago, just after he retired, and he told me they were pretty certain there was an Oxford spy-ring as well as a Cambridge one. There was a Labour MP called Bernard Floud who was a strong suspect, till he committed suicide in, I think, 1967."

"Didn't Peter Wright say something about it in his book that so infuriated the authorities a couple of years ago?" asked Dan.

"Yes, I think he did. I'm glad I never really got involved in the espionage business, though I know it was important," said Daniel. "Ted used to tell me that he didn't really enjoy his job."

"What annoys me is the way the recent revelations in the media have tended to glamorize the nasty little spies – people like Hamberly and Philby," said Ruth. "They claimed to have altruistic motives for their misdeeds, but between them they caused the deaths of a lot of people. They

109

may even have lengthened the time it's taken for the Russians to get to the hopeful place they've arrived at this year."

"There seems to be a recurring tendency among some British intellectuals to fall for the appeal of homicidal dictators if they claim to be representing the interests of 'The People'," said Dan. "I suppose Orwell was the first to draw attention to it."

"It goes back a lot farther than that," said Ruth. "When I was researching the Humboldt book I accidentally came across a wonderful quotation from Goethe. He was commenting on Lord Byron, who'd said he had contemplated suicide when he heard about Napoleon's defeat at Waterloo. Goethe said, 'He's great only as a poet. As soon as he reflects he is a child.' It sounds even better in German."

"That just about sums it up," said Dan. "A lot of very clever people seem to be incapable of thinking realistically about political issues. I think maybe vanity has something to do with it."

"Are you going to have a little celebration on the day when the Queen gives you your gong?" asked Ruth.

Dan gave a wry smile. "I hope it wasn't the mention of vanity that prompted your question. Actually, Mam and Dad are organizing lunch. You know how fond they are of celebratory meals, and you can be quite certain that your names are at the top of the invitation list. But I've been thinking it's high time you were given some recognition, Ruth. All those overseas sales of your books in Germany and America and Australia must have made a nice little contribution to the balance of payments over the years."

Ruth laughed. "I very much doubt if they brought any noticeable comfort to the Treasury. I'm happy if I've given some pleasure and a little bit of understanding to the people who've read them; and they've paid for a few things that we've enjoyed. Beyond that, I think Daddy is the only person whose face I would love to have seen light up if they'd given me a gong while he was still alive."

And I would have liked to be taking Dorcas with me to the Palace, Dan thought. A couple of lines by Byron flashed into his mind:...*to see the bright eyes of the dear one discover/She thought that I was not unworthy to love her.* But he kept his thoughts to himself.

CHAPTER FIFTEEN March, 1990

As the taxi drew up at the end of Birdcage Walk the driver asked, "You getting a medal for bravery?"

"Afraid not – just for having a good idea," Dan replied. He gave the man a one pound tip on the eight pound fare from Marylebone, and walked across to the Palace gates with his parents, whom he had earlier picked up from their home.

"I wonder if I'm going to be the only one without a hat," said Margarita.

"You're not. Those two girls with the man in naval uniform aren't wearing any," Arthur reassured her.

Dan looked at the throng of people in the Palace forecourt to see if anyone else was wearing a lounge suit. He would have been hard pressed to explain exactly why he had opted out of hiring morning dress for the occasion, but it had something to do with not wanting to take his investiture too personally, since it was partly a tribute to the achievements of other people; and he also had a long-standing aversion to 'dressing up'. He was relieved to spot a dark blue suit among the throng of grey and black tailcoats passing through the archway into the Quadrangle.

There was a separate entrance to the Palace for those who had come as spectators. As they parted Margarita kissed him on both cheeks. "It reminds me a bit of school Speech Days," said Arthur, patting him on the shoulder. "See you after you've collected your gong."

As he walked up the Grand Staircase between troopers of the Blues and Royals in gleaming cuirasses and scarlet-plumed helmets Dan reflected that what he was now engaged in was a State occasion. From that moment he took pleasure in observing the precision with which every stage of the event was organized. When he entered the Picture Gallery he was quietly directed towards a cluster of people on the left, and noticed that recipients of the MBE were being directed to the right.

He guessed that, as with all State occasions, waiting around was going to be the largest single element in the experience. However, it would be no hardship to wait in a space that was hung with some of the world's greatest paintings, and he quickly began to study the originals of pictures which he had so often seen reproduced in books on art.

While he was standing in front of Rembrandt's 'The Shipbuilder and his Wife' a voice behind him said, "He really gives you the sense of a working partnership, doesn't he? I love Rembrandt."

He turned around to see a smiling woman in a smart, cream-coloured suit, the colour of which enhanced her olive-skinned complexion. She was hatless and dark-haired, and her brown eyes sparkled with youthful enthusiasm, although he guessed that she must be at least in her late thirties.

"I do, too," he replied. "I was getting quite carried away. I'd almost forgotten why we're here."

"Why are *you* here?" she asked; and he explained, trying to keep the description of WHEN as brief as he could.

"And what have you done to bring *you* here?" he then enquired.

"I'm a nutritionist. I've been working with UNHCR – you know, the refugee agency. When people are refugees they often have to eat food that isn't what they've been used to, and that can cause all kinds of problems. I was trying to find answers to some of them, mainly in Africa. Unfortunately I got malaria last year and I had to pack it in. So now I'm doing research at the School of Hygiene and Tropical Medicine. It's a much quieter life, but not so exciting." She laughed, displaying a row of gleaming white teeth.

"That's very interesting," said Dan. "My day job is concerned with development issues, especially getting the private sector more involved. I'd be interested to hear more about what you've seen of the refugee situation. It isn't getting any better, is it? Maybe we could meet one day when there would be more time to talk – I think that military gentleman is about to address us." He nodded in the direction of a tall officer resplendent in court uniform, who had just appeared. Then, reaching into his jacket pocket, he handed her one of his cards. "I'm in London, too, as you can see. Maybe we could have lunch one day."

"That's a good idea. I think I have a card with me." She looked in her small, black handbag and quickly found one. He saw that her name was Laura Holmes – followed by DMSc, which he guessed must stand for Doctor of Medical Science.

"I'll give you a ring to see if we can arrange a meeting," he said, as they moved to join the semi-circle assembling around the official.

The investiture would be carried out by Her Majesty The Queen, he informed them, and all they had to do was to relax and enjoy it. They would be divided into groups of about a dozen, in which they would 'wiggle through' a series of rooms until they reached the State Ballroom, where the action was taking place. At a side entrance their names would be checked again, and they would then wait there until they heard the Lord Chamberlain read out their name.

The official then demonstrated exactly how they should move forward, turn, bow and move up to the low dais where the Queen would be standing. She would attach the decoration to their chest, speak to them briefly and then shake hands. "The handshake, I'm afraid, is the indication that your time is up." After that it would be four paces backward, bow, turn and walk off through another side door. Outside the decoration would be removed and put into a box to take away. Someone would be there to indicate the route by which they could discreetly rejoin their friends or relations sitting in the Ballroom observing the proceedings.

The instructions having been given, the waiting process was resumed. Divided into groups, they began a gradual movement through a series of sumptuously decorated rooms. Since Doctor Holmes came next to him in alphabetical order Dan was able to walk with her and resume their conversation. He learned that her mother was Greek, and during the Second World War had escaped to Egypt as a refugee. There she had met, and eventually married, a British naval officer.

"My father was based in Egypt for a time during the War," said Dan. "He was on General Montgomery's staff. He might even have met your father."

She laughed. "Stranger coincidences have happened." She went on to say that her dual nationality had given her a strong sense of history, and she proceeded to question him about the activities of WHEN, confessing that she knew very little about the history of countries outside Europe.

As they passed into yet another room she exclaimed *sotto voce* "Isn't that Penelope Keith in the group behind us?"

"Oh, yes," said Dan. "I remember seeing her picture in a report on the New Year list. She's a wonderful actress – ideal for the part she had in *The Good Life*."

"I used to think about that programme sometimes when I was in Africa," she said. "I was surrounded by people whose real need was to be able to stop having to rely completely on their own plots of land that provided them with a miserable, monotonous way of life. It might be fun to watch people trying to be 'self-sufficient' in a London suburban garden, but that's not something people should be aiming at in the real world. We just have to accept that we're all interdependent with one another. But I enjoyed the television programme and I agree that she's a great actress."

"You're absolutely right about interdependence," said Dan. "In a way, it's what my day job is all about. I once wrote a letter to *The Times* in response to someone who'd been banging on about self-sufficiency. I think I said it was not by renouncing the Industrial Revolution but by refining it that we would extend its benefits – which we now lightly take for granted – to another billion people."

She laughed. "If I'd seen that letter I'd have written myself to support you. But I think you're about to go through for the big moment. Thanks so much for talking to me. I was quite nervous when I arrived here but you've helped me to get over it. Enjoy the rest of your day." She shook his hand, and he noticed that her left hand was devoid of rings.

It then all happened exactly as predicted. The Queen looked smaller than she did on television as he walked towards her, turned and bowed, remembering that a British bow was a simple inclination of the neck, indicating respect but not servility. As he stepped towards the dais she was given the silver-gilt cross with a rose pink ribbon edged with grey, and she hooked it on to the holder that the official by the door had attached to his breast pocket. In how many countries was the Network now active, she asked, sounding as if she had always been aware of its existence. He replied that they now had members in nine countries, adding that five of them were in the Commonwealth, because he thought that might be of particular interest to her. She expressed the hope that its valuable work would continue to expand and then, smiling warmly, she extended her hand and he touched it lightly.

Having successfully stepped backward, bowed and turned, he walked off feeling that he was playing a miniscule part in one of those pageants that provided brightly coloured dust-jackets for children's history books. Outside the door he was relieved of the medal-holder, and his OBE was placed in a small black box, which fitted into his pocket. He was then directed back to the Ballroom by a circuitous route and found a seat across the aisle from where his parents were sitting.

As he sat down he noticed that Doctor Holmes had just received her decoration. When she stepped back and curtsied he observed the dip and rise of a very attractive bottom.

After the last medal had been pinned and the last hand shaken the National Anthem was played by the Guards band seated in the gallery. The Queen left the room, followed by two Gurkha orderlies (who were there, he knew, as part of a tradition instituted by Queen Victoria) and five Yeoman of the Guard in a glitter of gleaming partisans and red and gold Tudor uniforms. Dan rejoined his parents to walk with them down the Grand Staircase between the ranks of the Blues and Royals.

* * *

The organizing of the celebratory lunch had been taken over by his old friend Leo, who was, of course, President of WHEN. Four members of the Council and Sara Hoskins, the Co-ordinator, in addition to Leo's mother, Nancy, and his parents' other old friends, Daniel and Ruth and Rod and Rebecca had been invited. Leo had taken advantage of his rank to hire a room at the House of Lords for the occasion.

The mood was relaxed and convivial. Dan had insisted that there should be no congratulatory speeches, because the award had been as much for WHEN as for him. He expected there would be some jokes about getting taken over by the Establishment, and the first one came from Council member Veronica, who was a professor at the Institute of Education.

"Are you concerned that people are going to ask you if you're now 'Owned By the Establishment'?" she enquired.

"Not really," he replied. "Anybody who suggests that doesn't really know much about the Honours system."

"But don't you think the Honours system may soon have outlived its usefulness?" she persisted. "There was a time, I suppose, when people – especially civil servants – were willing to work for less money than they were really worth in the expectation that eventually they'd get a handle to their name, but I wonder if that's still true today."

"I'm sure it has always been an unspoken assumption where civil servants are concerned," said Dan, "But I'd be surprised if it has ever been very effective. For one thing, the odds against being selected for an honour are much too long, apart from a few small groups like ambassadors and permanent secretaries. I suppose they're the ones most likely to see the system as an inducement to stick with an unrewarding job. But for people like me, which I think includes most of the people at the Palace this morning, it would make no sense to slog your guts out in the hope that you might one day be selected to receive a bit of tin on the end of a ribbon." He tapped the black box on the table in front of him.

"Don't you think the roots of the ritual probably go down very deep into the foundations of society?" asked Ruth. "Handing out colourful tokens is a nation's way of signalling the kinds of behaviour it approves of. It's the opposite side of the coin from what the law courts do. They signal the kind of behaviour that the nation disapproves of. And just as only a small proportion of wrongdoers actually get caught and punished, so only a small proportion of those who do what's praiseworthy get publicly rewarded. It's not the rewards that really matter: it's the signals that they send out."

"I'm sure you're right," said Dan, "and that's why I think it's a disgrace when sometimes top honours, like peerages or knighthoods are given to people whose behaviour isn't praiseworthy, but who've simply made a big donation to the party or swung the trade union's block vote behind a party leadership candidate."

"Not mentioning any names," said Leo, "but I think I could if you pressed me to."

As Dan sipped his coffee he reflected that Ruth's theory had resolved a problem which had been troubling him – just a little – since the letter from Downing Street had landed on his doormat.

CHAPTER SIXTEEN April, 1990

As Anne handed Dan the list of businessmen who had accepted invitations to the 'working lunch' with the Minister for Overseas Development she remarked, "We'd better double check the menu to make sure it doesn't include anything that involves fussy eating. Like you said – we have to keep the emphasis on the conversation, not the food."

"So no spaghetti?" he said, smiling. "But you're quite right. I'm sure you can sort that out with your contact at the RAC. They were very good last time. Next week I'll ring a few people to make sure there are some pertinent questions lined up for her when she's finished her after-dinner speech – not that there's likely to be a problem with this lot." He tapped the list of names. "There are a few good talkers among them."

"Do you think we ought to do a lunch with the Shadow Minister some time?" Anne asked. "Everybody seems to think there'll be an election by next year and we could have a new government."

"I'd be very surprised if Mrs Thatcher would go to the country before she has to, and that would be in '92. The riots last week may have been whipped up by agitators, I know, but they weren't exactly a sign of public enthusiasm, and the opinion polls aren't where she would want them to be. I think she'll bide her time. But I agree it would be good to get Ann Clwyd involved at an early stage, while she's still thinking about her tactics in her new job. It looks as if Mr Kinnock is getting round to the idea that he needs to support the wealth creators if he's going to have the money he needs for all the things he wants to do. So it might help if somebody in his Front Bench team met a few wealth creators."

"That's not something that Lynda Chalker needs, is it? Didn't she use to work at Shell before she went into politics?"

"I think she did. It's the wealth creators who need to meet *her*, and it's good that we've been able to arrange it. There's another meeting I'm thinking about at the moment, for the journalists' group. Could you check out two or three possible dates after Easter, please? I'm going to have lunch on Monday with somebody I think might be an interesting speaker for them, and if she agrees I'll try to settle the date with her then."

"We seem to be having an all-woman line-up in the diary," said Anne, smiling. "Have I heard of this lady?"

"You haven't. I met her at Buckingham Palace. How's that for name-dropping? Actually, she was next to me in the queue to collect our gongs. I found out that she's done interesting work on the special nutritional needs of refugees, and I think there might be a discussion piece in it for some of them. The fact that she's just been given an OBE could give someone a peg to hang the story on. But I'll find out how she feels about the idea on Monday."

"What's her name?"

"Dr Laura Holmes. She's doing research at the London School of Hygiene and Tropical Medicine."

"Is she married?"

"I don't think so. She wasn't wearing a ring."

Anne smiled and picked up her papers. "I'll have a look through the diary and let you know what times are available. We'd better avoid anything too close to your DANEC committee meeting in Aachen. If she agrees to talk maybe I'll have the pleasure of meeting her."

* * *

It was the final day of the Frans Hals exhibition at the Royal Academy and Dan regretted that he hadn't visited it earlier. A lot of people who, like himself, had postponed their opportunity to see the pictures until the last minute were crowded into the gallery, making it difficult to get close enough to read the captions. However, he had bought a copy of the heavy, 400-page catalogue, and whenever an empty seat appeared he sat down and read about the next group of paintings he was about to encounter.

The unashamedly arrogant full-length portrait of Willem van Heythuysen caught his attention, and he read with interest the two-page account of its history and provenance. The elegantly black-costumed figure, one hand on a hip and the other leaning on a long, sheathed sword, was strangely enigmatic. The holder of the sword had no military connections, and the sternly puritanical black of his costume was contradicted by the luxurious lace of his flamboyant ruff and on the cuffs that covered his forearms. In a way, Dan reflected, he was symbolic of his country which, in spite of persistent warfare and scant natural resources, was at that very time becoming the wealthiest in Europe. Its embrace of a new capitalism and an aggressive maritime policy had raised the majority of its people out of medieval poverty to an unprecedented level of domestic comfort. And presumably Willem had celebrated his own rôle in that process by having his portrait painted – though he had instructed Hals to include *memento mori* symbols in the painting, which long after his death had found its way to a gallery in Munich.

In the last room of the exhibition Dan caught a glimpse, over the heads of the jostling throng, of two large pictures which instantly called up a poignant memory. They were the *Regents* and *Regentesses of the Old Men's Almshouse*. He had last seen them when the Frans Halsmuseum in Haarlem was open for a special 'candle-lit evening'. On holiday in Amsterdam, he had gone there with Catherine and, although his wife was not usually enthusiastic about art galleries, she had thoroughly enjoyed the experience. Looking up at the five black-suited, white-collared philanthropists, all wearing their broad-brimmed hats as they sat around a small table, he reflected that it was much more satisfying to look at pictures in company with someone else who wanted to discuss them.

When he emerged from the exhibition he decided against having a coffee in the restaurant and headed down the stairs to the main entrance. Among the throng of people coming through the doors towards him he recognized a face. It was Dr Laura Holmes. As she came closer he could see that she was casually dressed in a blue anorak and jeans, and she was accompanied by a slightly taller, fair-haired woman with a face that he instinctively classified as 'handsome' rather than 'beautiful'.

Almost immediately Laura caught sight of him and moved across to speak. "Have you just been to the Frans Hals?" she asked.

"Yes. I suddenly remembered this was the closing day. It's well worth a visit, but it is very crowded."

"We'd also forgotten about it coming to an end, and we'd twice postponed our visit. Then Daphne spotted an item in the *Observer* that reminded us. So we put on our coats and came. Oh, this is Daphne Wellesy, my…" There was a slight hesitation and then she continued, "my partner."

Dad did his best to conceal his surprise, smiling as he extended his hand and said, "Nice to meet you. I think you'll enjoy the exhibition." And, turning to Laura, he said, "We seem to keep meeting in art galleries."

"Yes. I told Daphne about our encounter at the Palace," she responded. "I'm looking forward to having lunch tomorrow."

"I have what I hope you'll find an interesting suggestion to make," said Dan, "but I mustn't delay you now. The exhibition's already very full. I'll be interested to hear tomorrow what you think of it."

He smiled again at Daphne and continued on his way to the exit. As he descended the steps into the Burlington House courtyard he reflected that this chance encounter might well have saved him a great deal of wasted effort that could have ended in a bitter disappointment. And once again he experienced an urgent desire to find someone else with whom to share his pleasures.

CHAPTER SEVENTEEN 11-12 May, 1990

Mistakenly going from Brussels airport to Central railway station, instead of to Noord, had added a couple of hours to the journey, and dusk was falling when Dan, in company with Fred Winter, arrived in Aachen. It was only a short taxi ride to their hotel, close to the historic Marschiertor city gate, and when they arrived they found their four fellow-members of the DANEC executive committee preparing to leave for dinner.

"We thought your flight might have been delayed, as flights so often are," said Kurt who, as an Aachen resident, had made the arrangements for the meeting. "I had just told the receptionist where we were going to eat, but now we can wait while you check into your rooms."

It did not take them long to walk to the restaurant which Kurt had chosen – on the grounds, he said, that it was a typical Rhineland Bierkeller. And he added proudly that Aachen had more restaurants than any other city in West Germany. Dan was happy to relax in the lively surroundings, although his private preference would have been to eat in an atmosphere more conducive to conversation.

When the soup arrived he asked Aisling Maguire, who was sitting on his left, whether there had been any DANEC activities in Ireland since he had last seen her, at the conference in Perugia.

"In February we had a seminar in Cork on 'Teaching Attitudes and Values'," she replied. "It attracted a wee bit of controversy. Some of the religious, who still play a big part in education on our side of the water, tend to think that they have a monopoly on teaching about values. The shenanigans were actually a bit of a sideshow, but you'd be surprised how many people are still trying to come to terms with Vatican Two."

"Are there many fans of 'Liberation Theology' in Ireland?" Dan asked.

"I think most of them are involved in 'Development Education'. And of course there are still a few Irish missionaries in South America; so there's a bit of a two-way traffic in ideas. But I think it's among a fairly select few.

Nowadays you'll see more bright young fellows heading off to work in Brussels than competing for a place in a seminary in Rome."

"I think you will see the same trend in Italy," said Franco Bonici, who was sitting on the opposite side of the table. "When I was at school there were still a few recruits lining up for the priesthood, but now I never hear of one. But of course some of the people in religious organizations that are part of our network are enthusiastic about 'Liberation Theology'. They've had conferences to talk about it."

"Have you ever met again with the lady from one of those organizations who did translating for us in Perugia? She was a contessa, I seem to remember," Dan asked, trying to sound casual.

"The Contessa Urbisaglia? No, I haven't seen her since Perugia; but then we haven't had any need for an interpreter. I have actually heard a few rumours – but about her husband, not about her. He's in politics, and in Italy there are always rumours about people in politics. But I hope they weren't true. They were not just about politics, and it sounded like he is not a nice person."

"I'm sorry to hear that – for her sake," said Dan.

"So am I," said Aisling. "I had a chat with her in Perugia and I formed the impression she was a really good-hearted woman."

"I am afraid that in Italy politics often seems to have a corrupting influence on people who go into it," said Franco. "Last year we made big changes in the Code of Criminal Procedure which should make it easier to bring the offenders to justice, but until now I haven't seen any sign that the police are taking advantage of the new law."

"Italy's not the only place where that happens," said Aisling. "We've had our share of scandals."

Dan decided it was time to change the subject. "What time have you arranged for us to start the meeting tomorrow morning, Kurt?" he asked. "A Teutonic seven o'clock, I suppose."

"I thought I should make allowance for the less industrious lifestyles of our fellow-Europeans," Kurt replied with a smile. "We begin at nine

124

o'clock. But you will need to leave your hotel by about eight-thirty in order to get to the meeting-room on time."

* * *

The main business at the first session of the committee was a discussion on the venue for the DANEC 1991 Conference. Dan discovered that the Joint Secretaries had already undertaken a lot of informal consultation, and the most attractive offer to host seemed to have come from the Netherlands branch. "They would have access to a very attractive conference venue in the Hague," Fred explained, "and accommodation in Scheveningen, which is not far away, would be fairly inexpensive. For energetic types it would even be within walking distance."

"The only other serious offer came from Spain," said Kurt. "Our friend Jaume said he was sure the provincial government would be willing to provide a venue in Barcelona; but I got the impression there might be some Catalan separatist propaganda involved in the package."

"Jaume is very passionate – about his Catalan nationalism," said Kirsten. "He does get a little carried away sometimes. It was good that he was willing to host the conference but I'm not sure he has enough people to make it work easily. As you know, I've met the Barcelona group and they're great fun, but they've not had much experience just yet."

"So you would be in favour of going with the Dutch?" Dan asked.

"Yes. I think for all our branches the Hague would be a very convenient venue for travel. And we might be able to persuade someone from the Secretariat in Brussels to look in for an afternoon."

Everyone was in agreement; and they proceeded to set up a planning committee to work out the details of programme and agenda. "Shall we ask Jan Brouwers to chair the committee and bring its proposals to our September meeting for final agreement?" asked Dan. "Kurt and Fred will be working with him, and maybe Franco, you would be able to give them the benefit of your experience in organizing Perugia, if you're willing to make a trip to the Netherlands."

"That would not be a hardship," said Franco. "Is there money in the budget for Planning Committee fares?"

"The funds are OK at the moment," said Fred, "but I'll need to talk to Brussels about the budget for the conference. I'll do that on my way home, on Monday."

The remainder of the morning agenda had been dealt with by midday, and they then adjourned for lunch to a nearby Greek restaurant. "DANEC has only three members in Greece, but we have to look to the future," Kurt joked.

"If we're looking to the future, I wonder if we might hope that the 1993 conference might be held in somewhere like Dresden or Leipzig," said Kirsten, as they took their seats around the table.

"Are you thinking that we'll actually have had our reunification by then?" Kurt asked.

"Well, Chancellor Kohl seems very determined to bring it about, and don't you think he is the kind of person who is good at getting what he wants?" she responded.

"Yes, I do – even though I didn't vote for him," said Kurt. "He's already produced a treaty for monetary and economic union that is probably going to be signed next week. I never thought we could move so quickly, but I guess the GDR economy was about to collapse. Their propagandists had been good at pretending everything was all right, when in fact I think their infrastructure was nearly collapsing. So I suppose that's why Kohl's offer was welcomed. If things have settled down by 1993 it would be a great idea to have the conference somewhere in the East – assuming that we've been able to recruit some DANEC members there."

"I see that Mrs Thatcher's not too happy about German reunification," said Aisling. "Apparently she thinks that Germany could become too strong and start being a threat to the rest of us again."

"She should come and meet the new generation of Germans. I think she would then not be so worried," said Kurt.

"You could have an opposite problem, like we have in Italy," said Franco. "If you have one part of the country that is used to depending on government hand-outs it can weaken the whole economy. Some people are starting to say that we ought to make the Mezzorgiorno into a separate

126

country and let them sort out their own problems. Brussels already gives them a lot of money, and half of it goes to the mafia."

"Do you think that idea will ever get serious political backing?" Dan asked.

"Wherever you have discontent you can be sure there will be politicians who use it for their own purpose," Franco replied. "Already there are some regional parties, like Lega Lombarda and Liga Veneta, that are flirting with the idea. Now that the Communist Party is in disarray strange things could happen in Italian politics. And of course the Christian Democrats are not in a much better shape – so many rumours about corruption. I think your politics in Germany are very simple in comparison with ours."

* * *

The afternoon session of the committee looked at a proposal for a publicity leaflet that would describe what DANEC had to offer potential members. There was a choice between printing four separate leaflets, in French, German, English and Italian, or having one double-sized leaflet with each paragraph printed in the four languages. Eventually they decided on the latter, following Kirsten's observation that in some of the smaller countries different people might be fluent in one foreign language or in another.

'Any Other Business' was briskly dealt with, and Dan realized he had a couple of hours to spare before having to leave for the airport. He asked Kurt whether it might be possible to see inside the cathedral, with its famous Oktogon, built by Charlemagne in the 9th Century.

"Of course before you leave you must see the most important place in the history of European unity. It was in the cathedral that thirty-two of the Holy Roman Emperors were crowned. I will take you in my car. It is only a few minutes' drive," said Kurt.

So when the farewells had been said they got into Kurt's green Volkswagen and drove to the cathedral. Its architecture was mainly Gothic, with magnificent stained glass windows, but preserved at its heart was the eight-sided chapel that was once part of Charlemagne's palace. As Dan tried to imagine what it might have been like eleven hundred years ago, Kurt

127

remarked, "I think perhaps Charlemagne is one of those people whose mythology has been more important than his history. Everybody afterwards who has tried to unite Europe has claimed him as their model, even though they all had different ideas about how to do it."

"I think he's a bit like Alfred the Great in British history," said Dan. "He never personally achieved all that he wanted, and yet without his efforts and his example things would have been very different. We might even have had Danish as our national language. I suppose one of Charlemagne's most lasting achievements was to ensure that Latin survived as a language distinct from its successors like French, Spanish and Italian. Generations of schoolboys would have hated him for it, if they'd known."

"Yes. I think his religious interventions were more lasting than the political ones. It is a big stretch of imagination to call him founder of the European Community. Founder of feudalism perhaps."

"I suppose one lesson that might be drawn from the Carolingian period is that while armed force may be able to bring about unification it isn't, on its own, enough to maintain it," said Dan. "That could be taken as a good omen for the future of the EC, which hasn't come together because of conquest."

"That is true," said Kurt, as they walked around the Chapel to get a better view of the alleged Throne of Charlemagne, "but the Community was very much a result of reactions to the terrible suffering caused by the War – and the First War as well. When that fades into the past people will have to find new reasons for staying together, I think. Already many of my students have only very vague ideas about the War. Their parents do not wish to talk about it. They know about the Cold War because of things like the Wall, but now that is also coming to an end. I am afraid that people may begin to be inward looking again and forget that their prosperity was brought about by working with other countries."

"I share your concern," said Dan. "At the beginning I was opposed to joining the Common Market because I thought its main result might be to create a big, new protectionist bloc that would hinder the movement towards free trade in a globalized world economy. To some extent that has happened, I think, but the EC has also kept the potential to be a model for the wider breaking down of barriers. That's the direction I would like to see it going in."

"I would also," Kurt responded, "but I am not sure the politicians have given the people a lead in that direction. Every time a problem comes up that seems to be a conflict of interest – is that the phrase you use? – between national interest and the common good they decide that supporting national interest is the way to win votes at their next election. Do you think I am too cynical?"

"Not at all. You can see why it is the easier choice. And I am also afraid that in the long run the voters will have forgotten what their common interests are. If that happens the old nationalist fears and suspicions could reassert themselves. We need electorates with a better understanding of political realities – and I guess that's where DANEC makes its little contribution."

Kurt nodded. "It is a great encouragement to meet people from other countries who are making the same efforts. I am sure that we will soon find people in East Germany who have the same concerns as we do. Maybe then a DANEC conference in Dresden would be a real possibility."

"I would certainly vote for that," said Dan, glancing at his watch, "but I think now I had better be getting on my way back to London."

CHAPTER EIGHTEEN   20-21 May, 1989

Occasional gusts of wind lowered the temperature in the Warner Stand where Dan was sitting in the front row, sandwiched between his parents and Ruth and Daniel. "This is only the third time I've been to Lord's this season," he said, in reply to a question from Margarita. "Last weekend I was in Aachen. Was the match with Nottingham a good one?"

"It was a high scoring one," Arthur replied. "Middlesex were unlucky to lose. But Roseberry was the only big hitter, and Gatting was out for a duck. One-day matches seem to bring out a different set of skills."

"They do," said Ruth. "Last week Dessy Haynes was out for ten, but this time in his first innings he was within shouting distance of a double century."

"I notice Gatt isn't playing in this match. Is he conserving his energy for the Championship games?" Dan asked.

"I expect so – that and the Benson and Hedges games. There's a quarter final coming up in about ten days' time," Arthur replied.

"And of course we're still missing Angus Fraser. I hope he'll soon have recovered from the injury he got in the West Indies," said Ruth. "We have two great spinners in Emburey and Tufnell, but we don't have a fast bowler to match him."

Dan remembered how, in his boyhood, when his father had been away on business it had sometimes been Ruth who had taken him to Lord's to watch the play, and share with him her own enthusiasm for the game. On several occasions he had heard the story of how she had been with his father at the Oval when Len Hutton had hit his fabled three hundred and sixty-four. And once, while they were watching a Middlesex game, she had told him that his father had played brilliantly one Saturday before the War for the village club of which her father was president. They had been short of a man and she had persuaded Arthur to fill the gap. At the time he had wondered if there might have been something between her and his father – it was at a time before his mother had arrived in Britain. But if there had been something it clearly hadn't affected the unusually close relationship between the two families in subsequent years.

His musing was interrupted by his mother's voice. "Shall we have some lunch now, like we usually do before the players take their break?" Margarita asked.

There was agreement that they should eat now and be ready to have a walk on the pitch at lunchtime, if it was opened to the spectators. The small wicker hamper with which he was so familiar was set on the seat beside him, vacated by Ruth, who asked, "What have you brought for us today, Margarita?"

"I made some little Cornish pasties last night; and there are some nice little cherry tomatoes, small enough to pop in the mouth, so that you don't have to bite them and squirt the juice. And I got some strawberries at Waitrose."

"Strawberries before Wimbledon – that's a luxury," said Daniel.

* * *

When they had finished eating, and the players had come off to have their lunch, spectators were allowed to walk on the pitch – carefully avoiding the guarded wickets areas, of course. Around the edges several bat and ball games quickly developed, most of them involving fathers and sons. At school tomorrow morning there would be little boys boasting to their classmates, "I batted at Lord's yesterday." Dan remembered that his father had never indulged him in that way, probably because, as a Yorkshireman, cricket was for him an activity too serious to permit such frivolity.

They walked together in the direction of the new Compton and Edrich Stands, and Dan fell into step beside Daniel, who asked him about his visit to Aachen. "Was your German colleague optimistic about the prospect of reunification?" he enquired.

"He was pretty certain it was going to happen. We even talked about having our next but one international conference somewhere in the East, like Dresden or Leipzig. It might be a bit too early for them in 1993, but it's certainly worth thinking about. Even something small, like that, could help to create a sense of being back in the international community once again.

Incidentally, I heard on the radio that the Romanians are holding their free elections today."

"Yes. They're discovering a different kind of freedom from the variety that our fellow-travelling friends used to tell us they had been enjoying over the past forty-five years. I once heard a funny story that made that point very effectively. I quoted it a lot when I used to speak about NATO at public meetings after I left the Army," said Daniel.

"Can I hear it? Might come in useful," Dan asked.

"I used to tell the story in a Northern Ireland accent for additional effect," said Daniel. "It goes something like this. In Belfast's equivalent of Hyde Park Speakers' Corner a small crowd was being harangued by a rare exponent – in those parts – of the benefits that would accrue to his hearers if they could achieve a people's democratic soviet system of government. He said 'When youse get your freedom yez'll all be earning forty thousand a year.' Encouraged by a spattering of applause, he went on, 'When youse get your freedom youse'll be the ones drivin' around in Rolls Royces.' A couple of listeners gave him an ironic cheer and, searching for an ultimate symbol of affluence, he said, 'When youse get your freedom yez'll all be wearin' top hats.' Inevitably, there was an independent-minded individual in the crowd and he called out, 'I'd look a right eejit in a top hat. I don't want to wear a top hat.' Outraged at this ingratitude, the speaker turned to him and said, 'When youse get your freedom yez'll do what you're bloody well told.'"

Dan chuckled. "That just about encapsulates the experience of a frighteningly large proportion of humanity over the past fifty years. Let's hope that for most of them the nightmare's coming to an end now."

Ruth, who had overheard the end of their conversation, commented, "Let's hope so indeed, but I wouldn't be too optimistic. Learning how to live with freedom – real freedom – seems to take a generation or two. If only the international community could be better prepared to step in at an early stage to stop the thugs when they start taking people's freedom away from them."

"This could be our second chance to create that kind of system," said her husband, "but I don't see any sign that we're going to take it. It's still all too easy for politicians – with the help of the media – to persuade their voters that any international problem is just the concern of 'people in a far-away country about which we know little.' When later on the problem comes back and bites them they find somebody else to blame for not having dealt with it sooner – probably NATO or the UN, or the Americans, if they're not American politicians."

"I'm afraid we've never succeeded in what we were trying to do in UNA in the early days, to get people to understand that if we don't all act together the moment the peace is broken, then sooner or later there'll be no peace for anyone," said Ruth.

Dan nodded in agreement, saying, "Send not to know for whom the bell tolls. It tolls for thee."

"When Hemingway called his Spanish Civil War book *For Whom the Bell Tolls* it was already too late," said Daniel. "The thugs had been getting away with breaking the peace for several years by that time. At least in my generation we'd taken that lesson to heart when we went into Korea – a place that was as far away as you can get – and today we're reaping the reward. But every generation needs to keep that lesson in mind, and I'm not sure the present bunch of opinion-leaders isn't in danger of becoming complacent. I suppose a lot of them would say that's just an old soldier being nostalgic and not understanding how the world has changed."

A disembodied voice asked them to clear the pitch and return to their seats, as play was about to recommence. As they turned around Ruth said, "The fundamentals never change, do they? If people aren't made to play by the rules the game very quickly turns into something nasty, and everybody suffers. That's the reason we should never send to know – it always tolls for us."

* * *

On Monday morning there was nothing of interest in the post; and when Dan had checked the diary with Anne – discovering that the week contained no important engagements – and enquired about the well-being of baby Alan, he decided to have a quick glance through the newspapers. As usual, the *Financial Times* and *The Times* were at the bottom of his 'In' tray.

He began his usual cursory survey of the newspapers, looking out for headlines that might indicate a story of particular interest. Agriculture minister John Gummer's 'photo opportunity' attempt to convince the public that eating British beef carried no risk of contracting 'mad cow disease' by feeding a beefburger to his little daughter was still provoking an outcry that looked as if it might have the opposite result. The Romanian election result was more encouraging than predicted.

As he flipped over a page a news item near the bottom caught his eye. *Arrests in Italy* said the headline. Quickly he scanned the short report, which said that early on Sunday morning police had arrested four prominent members of the Christian Democrat party. Two were members of parliament, one was a senator and the fourth was a senior office-holder in the party, responsible for fundraising. All were being charged with corruption, including bribery of the financial police, and it was rumoured that there were mafia connections. The accused were due to face a magistrate this morning, and an unidentified source had said that because of the mafia connection immediate bail was unlikely to be granted – possibly for the suspects' own protection. The names of the accused were listed, and the fourth leapt out of the page as Dan's eyes moved down towards it – Count Urbisaglia.

For several minutes he sat with his chin resting on his hand as he pondered the implications. Then he opened a drawer and took out his diary for the previous year. Among the phone numbers listed at the back he found the one that he needed.

"Pronto," said a voice that sounded apprehensive, when he finally got through.

"Is that Gina?" he asked.

"Dan! I thought it was going to be a reporter from one of the newspapers."

"Have you had many of them?"

"I don't think they are very interested in me – at this moment. That might change when more of the evidence comes out. Why have you rung? You've seen about Guido in the news?"

"I have, and I want to be with you, Gina. Will you let me come, and we can talk about what you should do now? I have a suggestion to make – no strings attached – and I want to help you. But I don't want to talk about it on the phone. I need to see your face and you need to see mine. I can probably get a plane and be with you by this evening. Please let me come."

There was a long pause, and then she said, "Oh Dan, about an hour ago I was wishing I could talk to you, and I told myself that wasn't possible because of what I'd done. And you actually kept my phone number! Oh Dan, I do want to talk to you. There's nobody I can trust here. I just want to be out of it."

"I have some ideas about how you can do that, but we need to find the way that will be best for you. If I can't be with you by the time the sun is going down today I'll ring you again. Oh, by the way, do you have a bell on your front door?"

"Yes, of course. Why?"

"I'll ring it in a way that lets you know I'm not an unwanted caller. Shall we say three rings, a pause, and then two rings?"

"That sounds all right to me. It will be music to my ears."

"It's a tune I never thought I would be playing. See you this evening. Ciao."

"Ciao."

Dan replaced the receiver and then lifted it again and spoke to Anne. "Can you come in for a minute, please? I need you to work your magic."

When she entered with a notebook in hand he said, "I want to be in Rome by this evening. While I belt off home to get my passport and my toothbrush can you book me a seat on a plane from Heathrow? It had better be a one-way ticket, because I don't know exactly when or from where I'll be returning. Give me a minimum of two and a half hours to get to the check-in, starting from now. And I'll need to be able to collect the ticket at the airport. Can you ring me at home with the details?"

Her eyes widened with astonishment. "This has to be something big. Are you sure you don't want me to come with you – I quite fancy a spot of southern sunshine?"

"Afraid not, but thanks for the offer. It's big but it isn't business. Somebody's in trouble through no fault of their own, and I want to see if I can help. You'd better have my personal card number to pay with; and when the phone bill comes in let me know how much the call to Rome cost."

Anne looked thoughtful. "I don't want to be nosey," she said, "but is it the contessa who's in trouble?"

"It is, and I'll tell you about it when I get back. On Wednesday I'll give you a ring, just in case there's anything you need to check with me. And I'm expecting to be back in the office on Monday."

"I hope it all goes well," she said. "I'll do my best to get you there in time – like the Seventh Cavalry coming over the Seven Hills."

CHAPTER NINETEEN 21 May, 1990

Dan's faith in Anne's ability to perform miracles was fully justified, and the sun had not yet totally gone from the sky when he rang the bell of the front door and heard Gina's voice on the intercom. As he stepped into the hall she closed the door behind him and threw her arms around him, kissing him on both cheeks. But then she stepped back, as though not sure if her action had been appropriate. Dan, too, felt uncertain, but when he held out his arms she came to him and he kissed her gently on her lips.

"When I woke up this morning," she said, "I thought, 'Now I'm really alone'. And at first it felt as if that's what I'd been wanting to happen for a long time, but then I started thinking that being alone and being free aren't the same thing. What I'd been wanting was to be free, but I was lonely because I didn't know what to do with my freedom. And then you rang. I can't believe it."

"The suddenness of it all must have really thrown you," he said. "I don't want to rush you into anything you might regret later on, but when you're ready I want us to talk this problem through. I want to be part of the solution – if you'll let me."

She snuggled against him and said, "This is like a dream. But you're right: I need to think carefully. It's the whole of my future I have to decide. Things have happened since the time when I was with you, and they may make it easier. In October my mother died."

"Oh, I am sorry," said Dan, giving her a hug.

"I'm glad that she never knew about... what's just happened," said Gina. "She was proud that I'd married a papal count. The other thing that's happened is that Bruno has started his training to be a naval officer. His grandmother's brother was an admiral, and by all accounts he was an honourable man. I like to think he might provide a rôle model for Bruno when the present storm has passed on. I don't think his father has ever been around for long enough to have an important place in his thoughts."

"You could be right about that. I hope so," said Dan.

"But where is your suitcase? Haven't you brought anything with you to stay here?" Gina asked, detaching herself from his arms.

"I dropped it off at the hotel on my way here. My wonderful PA had booked it for me when she bought my air ticket. I didn't want to presume on your hospitality – mainly because I don't want to be seen to do anything that could complicate your plans later on."

She squeezed his arm. "Luckily I don't seem to be interesting to the media. Maybe the paparazzi are more interested in the mafia contacts angle on the story. I don't know; but I'm happy that nobody has tried to contact me today. At first I was afraid that somebody might want to interview me or take a photograph when I was leaving the house; so I stayed in all day. I was beginning to feel trapped. If Guido does get bail I think he'll go to his mother's house; but he might not even want it if there's a possibility that the mafia could have a reason for trying to shut his mouth. That has been known to happen. But I stopped worrying about his welfare a long time ago. Can we get out of here for a while? Oh, have you had anything to eat?"

"I had something on the plane. I'm not really hungry."

"Nor am I. Let's go for a walk up the hill."

She put on a denim jacket over her blue summer dress, and they went out together into the quiet street, where the long shadows of evening were making pools of darkness but the lights had not yet come on. As they turned into a connecting street and their steps began to take them up a steep incline she said, "This is the famous Aventine Hill. I often walk to the little park up here when I want to be on my own, but now," she said, putting her hand into his, "I'm glad that I'm walking with you."

Soon they came to a small piazza in which there was a church. She led him inside the vestibule and up to a massive wooden door with elaborately carved panels. "There's something I want to show you," she said. "This Church of Santa Sabrina was built in the Fifth Century, and it's been very well restored. But it's the door I wanted you to look at, and this panel in particular. The door was made in about 430 AD, and this little panel was one of the very first times that anybody represented the Crucifixion in art. Four hundred years after the event and it was the first time anyone made a picture of it. Isn't that a bit like someone today painting the first ever portrait of

William Shakespeare? Every time I pass this church I think about religious symbols and how they get to be chosen, and the strange power they can have, once people come to accept them."

Dan peered closely at the small panel, which was surrounded by others also depicting scenes from the Bible. The carving was unsophisticated but strongly modelled. It showed a long-haired, bearded man, clad only in a loincloth, flanked by two others about half his size. All three had their arms outstretched with elbows bent – but no crosses were depicted. The rudimentary background looked like the end of a building, possibly a church, with some kind of three-part framework topped by three triangles.

"I wonder what image Christians had in their minds in the four centuries before this was made," he said. "I've read that in early times there was a reluctance to put much stress on the Crucifixion because it drew attention to the Roman authorities' involvement in carrying out the killing. And I wonder what the thousands of Calvary pictures and carvings and crucifixes now in existence will mean to people who look at them with as little emotional involvement as we now look at that earliest of war memorials that we call the Elgin Marbles?"

"Well, whatever happens I hope they won't have created any new symbols of supernatural intervention to blind them from seeing the world as it really is," she replied.

"Or, worse still," said Dan, "Some new swastika or hammer and sickle to tempt people into thinking they've found a 'scientific' answer to all their problems. You're right about the power of symbols. They certainly start you thinking."

"There's another church near to here that also has something thought-provoking," she said. "It's called San Saba, but it's on the other side of that horribly busy road you must have seen on the way here, the Viale Aventino. The church was founded in the Seventh Century by a group of Palestinian monks who had escaped from the invading Arabs. It has some pieces that were actually made for them, although since then the church has been rebuilt two or three times. I have thought about it sometimes when acquaintances have been indulging in the fashionable rant about the iniquities of the Crusaders. Of course a lot of nasty things happened in the Crusades, like in every war, but I can't believe it was a happy time when the Muslims went storming into Palestine and those monks who came here ran away from them."

"It was about the same time that the Angles and Saxons were storming into Britain," said Dan. "I think after the lapse of a couple of generations it's time to forego the indulgence of blaming our ancestors for whatever they may have done wrong, and concentrate on doing things better ourselves. 'New occasions teach new duties, time makes ancient good uncouth' – that's a line from a poem written by an American called James R. Lowell, and I remember it probably because a Welshman called Thomas J. Williams set it to music and I've heard it sung. Isn't it interesting how poetry that rhymes or is set to music seems to be much easier to remember than anything else – and sticks in your memory even if you don't want it to?"

"That's true. When I was studying English Literature there were poems I found it easy to learn, and I think it helped quite a lot in my exams that I was able to recall them. I wonder if you know the one that goes:

> *I remember, I remember*
> *The house where I was born,*
> *The little window where the sun*
> *Came peeping in at dawn."*

"Oh, yes. Thomas Hood was the sentimentalist, wasn't he?"

"That's right. I quoted the whole poem when I was answering an exam question on the Romantics. I remember coining a phrase: 'the seductiveness of sentimentality'. For that paper I got very good marks. I'm sure that now I would have no idea how to answer the questions. Isn't it strange how much information we stuff into our brains so that we can pass examinations and how soon most if it is forgotten?"

"My experience was the same – I quickly forgot the information that I didn't have to go on using. But didn't you teach English Literature and need to go on using what you'd learnt?"

"I taught it for only a few years. Afterwards I did some part-time teaching, but that was only English Language. But I still remember the poems – and quite a lot about the books that I enjoyed reading. I think it's

140

important to make learning enjoyable whenever you can, because then what you learn is much more likely to stay in your mind."

"That's very true. I've always enjoyed learning history and much of that I'm still able to recall, whereas all the Latin grammar and most of the vocabulary has long gone."

As they talked Gina led him around the side of the church and through a door in a wall that bounded a small park. There were orange trees hung with unripe fruit, under which several amorous couples were sitting on the benches. They followed a path to one side, from which they were able to look down over the Tiber and see the lights coming on in the streets of the Trastevere.

"This place reminds me of the garden we walked out to that night in Perugia," said Gina. "I think that's why I've liked coming here so much."

He put his arm around her shoulders and said, "It's strange how we build up strong associations with particular places. Before I met you Rome for me brought back memories of a World Food Conference organized by FAO – young Sixties radicals shouting slogans to save the world, and shagging each other in the bushes near the Villa Borghese – mixed in with my excitement at seeing the ruins of antiquity for the first time. Like a lot of British boys who studied the Classics at school I was influenced by the ideals of Republican Rome – public duty, honour, respect for the law."

"You will have to tell me more about British politics," said Gina, "but I think they are simpler than the system we have here in Italy. I know things are starting to change here, but I wonder if they'll ever change very much." She shivered a little and leaned against him, saying, "Shall we start going back?"

They left the garden, crossed the large street and entered the smaller one by which they had come. "If we take a small detour by way of the piazza there's a news-stand at the corner which sells evening newspapers," said Gina. "Maybe we ought to see if the story is still running, or if some new scandal has grabbed the attention of the journalists."

When they came to the news-stand Gina said, "I'll buy a paper that I don't usually read. The *Paese Sera* has tended to support the Communists, so it's probably the one most likely to keep plugging the story."

She picked up a copy of the paper and handed a coin to the elderly man behind the counter, who greeted her genially. They walked on across the piazza to an empty seat on the edge of the garden area at the far side, where they sat down before opening the paper.

"*Maria Santissima!*" Gina exclaimed, as she looked at the headline.

"What is it?" asked Dan, as he looked over her shoulder and saw that the heading on the lead story contained the word 'sex'.

Anxiously scanning the print, she said, "They're claiming to have heard from a well-informed source – which probably means the police – that several of the men arrested on corruption charges have been implicated in organizing sexual orgies for mafia bosses in a villa near Naples."

"Do you think that's true?" he asked

"It wouldn't surprise me; but whether it's true or not, it's a story that's going to run with the media."

Dan nodded his head. "And if they want a picture to illustrate the story I have no doubt about which of the accused has the most photogenic wife. 'Did you know what your husband was up to, Contessa Urbisaglia?...' 'Are you going to stand by him when he goes on trial?' I can just hear the questions they will want to fire at you."

"Well, they're not going to receive any answers," said Gina, folding up the newspaper and placing it in the waste bin at the end of the seat. "I'm coming with you, wherever you want to take me."

"In the hope that you might say something like that, I worked out a plan while I was sitting in the plane this afternoon," said Dan. "I've heard that Rome Airport is notorious for paparazzi on constant look-out for stories; so I don't' think that would be a good option. Pisa would be a better bet, although now that we're in the height of the holiday season it could be a day or two before we managed to book seats to London. So my proposal is that we go first thing tomorrow morning to Siena, where I have an old

142

acquaintance who, I am sure, will put us up – he owns a small hotel – and he'll probably also be able to help with booking the plane tickets. Then we're off to London and you will have all the time you need to think about what you do next."

"How should we go tomorrow? I don't want to take the car."

"Let's get a very early train. I know we'll have to change at Chiusi, but we'll be travelling light. When you're packing tonight just concentrate on anything you don't want to leave behind – and the essentials, of course, like passport, credit cards, cheque book. I'll be more than happy to get you whatever you need in London. And if you finally decide to stay for good I'm sure we'll be able to find an appropriate time to pop back and collect anything you don't want to abandon. But I hope you're going to make a clean break, and as well as that I hope you'll let me help you to do it. Could you be ready to leave by about six o'clock tomorrow morning?"

She laughed. "As early as you like. I just want to be away as quickly as I can. Luckily I know a friendly taxi-driver who usually likes to pick up early arrivals at Termini. I'll phone him when I get home. Shall we meet on the little green at the front, just by the entrance to the Metro station?"

"I'll be there; but maybe we should walk in separately, without appearing to recognize each other, just in case there should be a camera around – though I doubt if any of the paparazzi are up that early in the morning. I'll have bought the train tickets already."

"I suppose I ought to be wary when I go home tonight, just in case one of them has been reading the *Paese Sera*," said Gina. "I'll use the rear entrance through the garden. I'll be fine walking home on my own. You can get back now to the hotel and have some sleep. The little street to your right leads into another piazza, and if you take the right fork downhill from there you'll come to the big Viale Aventino. It's not very far along there to the Circo Massimo station, right in front of the FAO building."

"I came up from there tonight," he said. "It's only two stops back to the hotel. But I think I might be too excited to get very much sleep tonight."

143

"We'll have a nice strong coffee on the train tomorrow morning," said Gina. Then she kissed him, quickly but firmly on his lips and walked away briskly across the piazza.

CHAPTER TWENTY 22 May, 1990

Facing each other in seats by a window, Dan and Gina watched the last straggling outposts of Roman suburbia pass them by as the train picked up speed. "I wouldn't be unhappy if I never saw this city again," said Gina.

"I wonder how many people have said just that over the centuries," said Dan. "When I've visited I've found lots of fascinating things to look at, but I've never developed an affection for this city, like I have for Venice and Florence and Siena."

"You said you've been to Siena several times."

"I have. And last night I phoned my old acquaintance, Luigi Pinto, and he said he would be delighted to help us – or words to that effect."

"That's great." Her face brightened and she asked, "How did you get to know him?"

"The first time I went to Siena – I think it was eight years ago – I stayed at his hotel. It's fairly small, but it has a very good restaurant attached to it. You'll see for yourself very soon. Nowadays he spends most of his time in the restaurant, because he enjoys it, and his son, Enrico, has taken over managing the hotel.

"Anyhow, one evening there weren't many people in the restaurant, I suppose because I prefer eating earlier rather than later, and we got talking. I'd noticed there were some Arsenal Football Club memorabilia on the walls and, although I'm not really a football fan, I've always supported the Arsenal. So we found we had an interest in common. And he told me he'd worked in London, as a waiter in a restaurant in Charlotte Street, about thirty years earlier.

"When I went back to Siena again, two years later, I naturally stayed at his hotel, the *Pantera*. We got talking again one evening and I mentioned that my Uncle Daniel had been in Italy during the War. Then Luigi told me that he'd joined the partisans when he was a teenager; and I asked him if he'd ever come across a chap called Isolani, who had been an army liaison officer with the partisans, and who was an acquaintance of Uncle Daniel's. I met him once when he was visiting London. He'd actually become a secret agent by then, although I didn't know that. He was British but his father had been an Italian count. Anyhow, Luigi actually remembered meeting him, and he told me a lot about Italy at the end of the War – and about his time in London. On my third visit to Siena Daniel and Ruth came with me, and it worked really well."

"You must know Siena very well, then," said Gina. "From its name I presume that the hotel is in the Contrada of the Panther."

"It is; but I wouldn't claim to know such a complex place as Siena any more than superficially. It's as much as I can do to remember the names of all the seventeen contrada. And I've never been there at the time when they compete against each other in their famous horse race, though I've promised myself – and Luigi – that one year I'll come and watch the Palio."

"I read a fascinating magazine article about Siena last year," said Gina. "Did you know that it has the lowest juvenile crime and drug abuse rate in Italy, and a low suicide rate, too? The writer, who was a sociologist, put it all down to the contrada system that creates small communities where everyone looks after everyone else; and the Palio gives them a valid reason for hating the people in the other contradas, because – according to the author – a community gains in its own cohesion by having external opponents who threaten it."

"That's interesting," said Dan. "I remember Uncle Daniel telling me that Northern Ireland, where he grew up, used to have the lowest crime rate in the UK. That was in the days before the present sectarian violence. He said it was because the two communities, Roman Catholic and Protestant, saw themselves in competition and paid a lot of attention to nurturing their young people. But I think he would admit that failing to move on from competition to co-operation has left them with a terrible price to pay."

"I don't think that's likely to happen in Siena," said Gina, "though I have heard that there can be violent incidents associated with the Palio. But it's not the guns and bombs type of violence."

"Well, from now on we will have to be supporters of the Panther," said Dan. "They have a very appropriate motto: 'My leap overcomes all obstacles'. I hope that's going to be true for us." Her hand was resting on the small folding table between them and he put his own hand on top of it, squeezing gently. She met his glance with a smile that suggested she was at ease, and they lapsed into a temporary silence, looking out of the window.

As he glanced at her lovely profile he was suddenly reminded that the urgent desire for physical intimacy which had been ever present with him during Gina's visit to London had not intruded on his thoughts since his arrival in Italy – but now it was beginning to stir. He told himself sternly that he must pay no heed to it until they had left behind the slightest possibility of prying eyes and ears. And even then he would have to wait until such time as Gina indicated she was ready to begin again where they had so reluctantly left off.

The problem of finding out to which platform at Chiusi they would need to hurry for their connecting train began to worry him; and then he reflected that there should be no problem finding someone ready to rush to the assistance of the beautiful woman sitting opposite him. He ought to relax and enjoy the journey in her company.

* * *

When they arrived in Siena they had no difficulty in finding a taxi to convey them up the steep hill from the station to the old city centre. Luigi was expecting them, and his welcome was warm and understanding. Mindful of the way in which gossip is generated, Dan had asked for separate rooms and separate accounts.

On their return to the hotel foyer after unpacking they talked to the receptionist, Carlotta, who was also well known to him from previous visits. She willingly agreed to do her best to book them seats on a flight to Heathrow – again, to be paid for individually.

"Now it is time for you to relax and enjoy being in Siena," said Luigi.

Dan saw his face light up with pleasure when Gina replied, "Thank you. It is one of my favourite places, and I don't think I could ever grow tired of it."

When they stepped outside into the glare of the late morning sunshine Gina asked, "Where shall we go?"

"If you are agreeable, I would like to have another look at my favourite work of art, even among all the magnificent pictures in this city," Dan replied.

"Let me guess. I bet it's the 'Good and Bad Government' frescoes by Lorenzetti. Am I right?"

"Yes, you are. When I was here about two years ago they had just completed the restoration. I think they did a good job on it. But because of all the publicity at that time there were a lot of people around and I promised myself I'd come back some time when the Sala della Pace was less crowded."

"Then that's where we ought to go," she said. "Do you know the way from here?"

"I think it's pretty straightforward. If we cross the piazza that's just ahead we'll go into the Via di Citta, and that will take us all the way to the edge of the Campo."

* * *

Crossing the huge semi-circular space around which the legendary horse race was run twice yearly left them feeling thirsty, for it afforded them no escape from the glare of the midday sun. So they found a little bar where they drank lemon soda standing at the counter before they went inside the gothic entrance to the Palazzo Pubblico.

"I remember now, it was a hot day like this when I climbed up these stairs to see the pictures," said Gina. "By the time I'd gone through the Anticappella and the Mappamondo room I was starting to feel exhausted, but I really perked up when I came to the Lorenzettis."

They resisted the temptation to linger in the rooms along the way, and soon they were standing in front of 'Effects of Good Government in the City'. It depicted the citizens going about their daily business and a circle of women dancing in the street, against a background of pink and grey houses, shops and towers. "This is the kind of scene I think people today in Romania or Poland might respond to with some emotion," said Gina. "You don't have to know a lot about history to be able to identify with what it's saying."

148

"Before I came here last time I read a book about the frescoes, written by an Italian professor," said Dan. "I can't remember much about it now, because it was incredibly detailed. There is so much symbolism in virtually everything that's portrayed in these pictures. For example, the arts and crafts are all represented, from the builders working on the roof, up there, to the teacher with his pupils, and the cobbler and the goldsmith. According to the professor the Council of Nine, who commissioned the frescoes, wanted to spell out the theory that everyone has a valued role in society – and ought to stick with it."

"That's fairly straightforward," said Gina, "but what about all those grotesque figures in the two 'Allegory' frescoes?"

They turned around to view the pictures on the two opposite walls. "That's where my memory fails me," said Dan, "because it's all very philosophical; and some of the figures are actually said to have more than one symbolic meaning. According to the professor, the 'Good Government Allegory' illustrates two Aristotelian concepts, Justice and the Common Good, as interpreted in a commentary by Saint Thomas Aquinas. The fact that a bunch of Fourteenth Century businessmen wanted to put that on the wall of their council room tells us a lot about life at that time – at least here in Italy."

"It might be no bad thing if our present-day Cabinet were to hold its meetings in this room," said Gina.

When they had done as much viewing as they could absorb they went back down the iron staircase and out into the blinding sunshine of the Campo. "Do you fancy a toasted ham and cheese sandwich?" Dan asked. "They do a good one at 'Nannini', which isn't far from here."

"I think I remember that *pasticceria*," Gina replied. "Yes. Let's go."

When they had finished their sandwiches and cappucini Gina said, "I'd love to stay in this private world of pleasure, but I suppose we really ought to check on whether… whether there have been any developments in the news. I can see a shop across the street that's selling newspapers."

"You stay here and I'll go across and get one," said Dan. "Which paper would be most likely to pick up anything on the scandal?"

"I suppose *Il Messagero* is the most likely."

Dan quickly returned to the table with a copy of the paper and handed it to her, glancing at the front page headline. "Is that headline saying Ion Iliescu's party won a big victory in yesterday's election in Romania?" he asked.

She scanned the article and replied, "Yes. His National Salvation Front got eighty-nine per cent of the votes, and there was a ninety per cent turnout. That's not bad for the first free election that they've ever had."

"I guess you could make a photo montage of the news pictures that came out of Romania after the Communist collapse and use it as a modern update of the 'Bad Government' fresco," said Dan.

"That's quite an idea. I would give a copy of it to every student with a Che Guevara poster on his bedroom wall, to hang alongside the image of their hero. There were a lot of those posters around when I was at university."

"I remember that some of my contemporaries preferred Chairman Mao as their icon," said Dan. "There's something grotesque about people thinking they were displaying their credentials as compassionate, freedom-loving, idealistic individuals by putting a picture of history's most destructive mass murderer on their walls."

"He was popular in Italy, too," said Gina, turning over the page of the newspaper. "Somebody is questioning whether the facilities are going to be ready in time for the FIFA World Cup that starts next month, here in Italy."

"I'm sure Luigi will have something to say about that," said Dan.

She turned over another page and he saw her stiffen as she looked at the headline and photograph on the reverse. "Oh no!" she exclaimed.

"What is it?" he asked, as she rapidly scanned the report.

"A prostitute has sold them a story about how she was paid to take part in an orgy at a house in Porto Ercole last year. She's named people who were there, including Guido; and the paper has published a photo from last year. It's not of the orgy, but of a Party fund-raising event in Rome, and it

150

shows three of the people accused in the corruption scandal, with their wives. Have a look."

She turned the page around for him to see the photograph. It was a self-consciously posed shot of six people against a palatial background. In the centre of the group was Gina, looking glamorous in a low-cut gown. Dan realized that the tall, distinguished-looking man at her left side had to be her husband, since the two other men were both much older.

"Well, at least it's not on the front page," he said.

"Can we go back to the hotel and find out if Carlotta has been able to book our flights?" she asked. "I want to be out of this country just as soon as I can."

"OK; but can I suggest a little detour that will take us back around the side of the Duomo? I'd like to have another glimpse of that black and white masterpiece of medieval architecture," said Dan, concerned that she shouldn't start worrying about the possible implications of the published photograph.

"Do you remember what happened the last time you took me on a detour?" she asked, getting up from the table.

"Yes. That was the night when we started on the journey that's brought us here today," said Dan. "I'll never forget it."

"It was the night when I rediscovered what it feels like to have hopes for the future. I'm not going to lose that feeling ever again." She slapped the newspaper down on the table and turned towards the door.

* * *

When they turned the corner into the Piazza del Duomo Dan looked up at the towering Gothic façade of the cathedral and remarked, "They were incredibly self-confident, those medieval Sienese. Did you know they were planning to build the biggest cathedral in the whole of Christendom? That huge blank wall beyond the campanile shows what the dimensions would have been if they hadn't had to abandon the project."

"It's very beautiful as it is," said Gina. "I love the black and white stripes."

"The building that impresses me most of all is the one on the opposite side of the piazza, but not for its appearance," said Dan.

"You mean the hospital?"

"Yes. It's incredible to think that the first hospital building on that site was put up in the Ninth Century. When you consider that in Britain it took us another eleven hundred years to get around to the National Health Service that surely says something about a community that was able to tackle its problems in such a practical way.

"But I'm as impatient as you are to find out when Carlotta has been able to get us a flight," he went on. "So shall we cut down the Via del Capitano and get back to the hotel?"

* * *

The moment they stepped inside the coolness of the hotel vestibule Carlotta called out to them. "Signor! Signor! I have booked the flights for you."

With delight they learned that they would have seats on an Alitalia flight to London the following morning. Dan was congratulating Carlotta on her achievement when Luigi, having heard their voices, came out of the office smiling broadly. "I will drive you to the airport myself," he said.

Dan protested that they would not want to take up so much of his time, but he insisted. "It is many months since I last looked at the Leaning Tower of Pisa," he joked, "and if the weather is like today it will be a pleasant drive."

Gina thanked him, and said, "I am looking forward to dinner this evening. Dan has told me so much about your wonderful restaurant."

Luigi's face widened into a beaming smile and he said, "I have for you reserved the Bob Wilson table."

She looked puzzled and Dan explained, "There's a secluded corner in the restaurant which has a signed photo of Bob Wilson – Arsenal's greatest ever goalkeeper – on the wall. It's the best table in the house."

"That's very kind of you," said Gina.

Luigi's smile became even wider. "On the menu tonight we have *ribollita al cavolo nero*. I remember that was a favourite for you," he said to Dan.

"Yes, indeed. It's a Tuscan bean soup," he explained to Gina, "but you probably know that."

"I didn't, as it happens; but I'm sure I'll enjoy it." She turned to Luigi and said, "I wish we could stay to have more of your dinners, but you can be sure that when my problems have been sorted out we'll be back again to work our way through the whole of your menu."

Suddenly Dan had the spine-tingling realization that the hope he had not been allowing himself to entertain might actually soon become a reality.

CHAPTER TWENTY-ONE 23 May, 1990

They set out from the hotel in Luigi's Fiat shortly after seven o'clock, when the sun was already quite high in the sky. Luigi told them, "I will not be using the *superstrada*. In theory it is the fastest route, but at this time of the year it will be crowded; and it has no emergency lane. We have plenty of time; so I will take you by roads that go through places more interesting to look at."

The first interesting place they came to was Monteriggioni, which Dan had visited by bus on his last trip to Siena. The road passed below the hill on which it stood, and Luigi remarked, "There aren't many villages that still have their medieval walls complete. There are fourteen towers and they were mentioned by Dante in his *Inferno* - not that I've read the book, but the tourist guides quote it."

A little farther along a side road forked off to the left, and Luigi said, "Down that road my cousin Guiseppe lives. He has a farm near Colle di Val d'Elsa – lots of olive trees. His father was cousin to my father, and he was wounded in Abyssinia. He was a… what's the word for somebody who is made to join the army?"

"A conscript," said Dan.

"That's it. When I was a small boy he told me stories about bad things that happened down there. The planes dropped mustard gas on the black men; and some of the Africans only had spears and swords to fight with. Mussolini just wanted something to make him look like Julius Caesar. I remember talking about it to Colonel Hardstaff when he was here with you. He said that if the big countries had stopped him through the… what's it called – like the United Nations?"

"The League of Nations," said Gina.

"Yes. If they'd stopped him then Hitler might not have tried to do the same kind of thing, and we might not have had the War."

"I've often talked to him, and to my father, about that time," said Dan. "They were both students then, but involved in politics. I remember my
154

father telling me that a lot of people in Britain were very upset about what was happening in Abyssinia but they didn't want to get into a war with Italy to stop it, because it was somewhere far away. And then when Hitler invaded Czechoslovakia the British prime minister said that place was a far away country we knew nothing about. And then a year or so later the bombs began to fall on London; and after that young men like you took up guns to get rid of Mussolini."

"It was on this very road, a few kilometres from here but on a fork we're not going to take today, that I got into my first ambush," said Luigi. "We were waiting behind the trees above the road to shoot up a German supply convoy, but it never came. Farther back, near Pisa, a Communist partisan group blew up a bridge when the first truck was on it. We were planning to shoot up the whole convoy. Later on your uncle's friend, Isolani, was one of the guys who organized a bit more co-operation, though it was never very good."

"When did the Allies get to Siena?" asked Gina.

"That was in Forty-four. Luckily the Germans had already cleared out and the city wasn't damaged. It was a Free French unit that came in to liberate Siena. I was still up in the hills, but we came down two days later to join in the celebrations."

Soon they were passing through the outskirts of another town, and Luigi said, "We're coming to Poggibonsi. It's a fairly big place but there's nothing worth looking at. A lot of the buildings were put up in the Fifties, when there wasn't much spare money around."

As they passed through the centre of the town Dan noted that there were, indeed, no buildings attractive to the eye. But soon they were out again in delightful rolling countryside.

"We'll soon be in Cortaldo," said Luigi. "The old town has some good buildings. Another famous author whose book I never read was born there. Boccaccio."

"I've read *The Decameron*," said Gina. "Parts of it are good fun. You should try it some time."

When they had passed through Cortaldo Luigi began talking about his time in London, and entertained them with stories about eccentric customers at the restaurant in Charlotte Street where he used to work. "Where did you live when you were in London?" Dan asked.

"For most of the time I had a room in a house owned by an Italian lady, in John Street. It's not far from the Italian Church in Clerkenwell, and she was always going to mass there."

"It's also not very far from where I live in Lamb's Conduit Street," said Dan. "Did you ever come across that street?"

"I remember the name, because it was a funny name for a street."

"You have a saying in English: 'It's a small world'," said Gina.

"We do," said Dan, "and I keep being reminded of it. Luigi, when you feel like a holiday you must come and see us in London, and we can look for places you used to know. I expect you won't be able to recognize some of them."

"You can give us your opinion on an Italian restaurant where Dan likes to eat," said Gina.

"Ah, so you also know London," said Luigi.

"Not really. I've just been there once," Gina replied, a little too hastily. "But nowadays everyone goes to London at some time, it seems. I hope you will come soon."

As the hills on either side of the road became less noticeable Luigi remarked, "We are going down now to the valley of the Arno river. The town in front of us is San Miniato. There was fighting here in the War and some of the buildings were badly damaged. The castle up there on the hill was nearly destroyed, but part of it has been restored now."

A little later Luigi said, "We're now on the old road between Florence and Pisa. It gets flatter along by the river, and there's a lot of industry down there. They make motor-scooters in Pontedera, the town we're coming to after the next bend."

"In Rome motor-scooters are a menace," said Gina. "Quite apart from the reckless driving, some youths employ them for handbag-snatching."

"I've heard about that," said Luigi. "We don't have any of it in Siena."

After Pontedera they came to Cascina which, Luigi told them, had a lot of little factories making furniture. "Soon now you'll see some of the planes arriving at Pisa," he said; and a few minutes later they caught a glimpse of a plane descending gradually in the sky ahead of them.

They had no problem finding a space in the airport car park, and Luigi insisted on walking with them to the terminal building. As they approached it Dan noticed that two men with cameras, one of them a videocam with microphone on top, were standing near the entrance.

"Do you think they have a regular paparazzi presence here?" he asked. "I can't believe that anyone would know about us." He saw that Gina's face had become anxious.

"Stay here," said Luigi. "I'll go and ask a question. Don't worry. I'll make it casual."

They watched as he approached the entrance and then pretended to notice the cameramen for the first time. He stopped and spoke to them, and there was a brief conversation which included some laughter.

Watching intently, Dan saw him put his hand behind his back and make a gesture indicating that they should go ahead. "I think it's OK," he said. "Let's join him inside."

Once they were inside the building Luigi rejoined them, smiling. "They're here to welcome back a schoolgirl from Poggibonsi who won a competition to design the symbol for a European schools project. She is on her way back from Brussels, where she's been collecting her award," he said.

"I'm glad the media sometimes take an interest in good news," said Dan. "Luigi, you've been a brilliant friend. I hope it won't be long before we see you in London. Telephone and let us know when you'd like to come."

"And when I've got things straightened out for the future you can be sure we'll make a longer visit to Siena," said Gina. "Thank you again." She kissed him lightly on both cheeks.

* * *

The flight was uneventful, with cloud preventing them from seeing anything of the ground below until they were over the Channel. After they had landed at Heathrow Dan said, "I don't normally do this, because public transport is reasonably good, but today I'm going to take a taxi back home. I can't promise you anything like the scenery we passed through on the way from Siena, but at last you can sit back and relax. Just enjoy the knowledge that you're away from the prying eyes and the prattling tongues."

"It's a great feeling," said Gina. "Tonight I must ring my sister Elena and let her know that I'm OK; but I'm not going to tell her yet where I am – just 'gone abroad'. That way if people start asking her where I am she won't have to lie to them. She's not a very good liar. I was better than her at that when we were kids." She laughed, and Dan was pleased to observe that it was a carefree laugh.

They didn't have long to wait for a taxi. As they settled in their seats Dan remarked, "This is known as a 'black cab', even though the one we're in happens to be a silvery colour."

"I'm going to enjoy learning all the things I need to know about living in London," she said.

"Maybe you could write a guide for Italian visitors in your spare time," he said. "There are plenty of things that might be specially interesting to Italians."

"I think the intelligent ones will want to know all about things that are peculiarly British," she replied. "They won't want to know about where to get spaghetti: they'll want to know where to find fish and chips."

"That gives me an idea," he said. "I think we might have fish and chips for lunch today."

When the cab moved onto the M4 and increased its speed they both fell silent for a time. Dan even began to feel himself starting to nod off, lulled by the steady hum of the engine, and turned his head sharply to look out of the window. He could see nothing of visual interest on which to comment, and so he said, "When my father was an MP his constituency was just a few miles to the north of here. I grew up in a very pleasant house there, but it wasn't the most exciting place in the world – certainly not for a teenager. I was perfectly happy, and yet from quite an early age I had a strong desire to get away and explore the wider world."

"I was just the same," said Gina. "I was quite happy growing up in Bassano, but I always knew it wasn't where I wanted to live."

"I'm afraid this isn't the most picturesque entrance to London," said Dan, as they sped on to the Chiswick Flyover, "but it does become more interesting quite soon."

"It's the destination that matters," said Gina. "You know what a dreary place Mestre is; but I always felt excited when the train arrived at Mestre on my way back to Venice at the end of university vacations. I loved my time in Venice, but even there in my last year I knew that I had to move on. It wasn't where I wanted to settle for good. Of course, I never intended to settle in Rome and yet that was where I ended up. I remember that my sister Elena always wanted to live in Bassano, and I think she's been very happy there."

"The world does seem to be made up of two kinds of people," said Dan. "Maybe it's in the genes. There are those who seem content to settle for familiar places and familiar faces, and the rest of us – a minority, I think – who go looking for something new."

"I suppose if it wasn't for the minority we'd still be living in caves and picking berries to make our diet more interesting," said Gina.

"Yes; and then, once the minority have found the way to pastures new it becomes the turn of the majority to make the new ways work – to do the boring business of sowing and reaping and milking the cows," Dan added. "We have a saying in English: 'It takes all kinds to make a world'."

Gina turned her head to look at him. "One of the things I've been missing all these years was having somebody to talk to about... ideas, like we're talking now. Oh, look! Isn't that the River Thames?"

"It is. I think this is the only glimpse you'll have of it today, but I guess you'll be seeing a lot more of it in the future. We'll soon be passing through a part of town where there's a lot of intellectual activity. We didn't get to any of the South Kensington museums when you were here last year, did we?"

"No. You kept saying that we must go to the Victoria and Albert, but we never managed to do it."

"There were so many things we wanted to do in that short time," said Dan. "Now there will be time for them all."

"I love getting to know places really well," she said. "I must have been in the Vatican museums about ten times, and there were still parts of them that I hadn't seen. And I think it can be the same with just one picture or one sculpture. You look at it again and you see something you hadn't seen the first time – maybe because you'd been so excited at actually getting to see it. Do you know the Michelangelo Pietà in St Peter's?"

"Yes, it's incredibly beautiful."

"I've gone back time and again to look at it, even though I don't like St Peter's – all that over-sized, bombastic Baroque. I admired the sculpture the first time I saw it because it seemed to say everything you could say about a mother mourning for her dead son. But it puzzled me, too, because Mary looked far too young to be Christ's mother. So I went to the library and read up about it, and I found out that when it first appeared – not in St Peter's, actually, but in Santa Petronella – other people had made the same comment. Apparently Michelangelo said he'd made her look like that because it was the only way he could portray her 'virginity and eternal purity'. He was only twenty-three when he did it. And I discovered that, although German and French sculptors had already done Pietàs, this was the first one in Italy; so he'd probably never seen one before."

"I think that explains why it's so different from his last Pietà, which happens to be one of my favourite sculptures," said Dan. "Do you remember the one in Florence, where he's made his self-portrait as Nicodemus supporting the dead Christ?"

"Yes, I know the one you mean. They say he intended it to go on his own tomb. I know that because the St Peter's statue got me really interested in Michelangelo and I went on to read a lot more about him. That's why I think it's so good to have the time to really get to know a work of art. I did it with a lot of them in Rome, and now I'll be able to do it in London."

"Just before we get to the V and A you'll see the Natural History Museum, and behind it is the Science Museum. Are you interested in them?"

"Yes, definitely. I don't know a lot about science and it's time I found out more. The only science I did at school was biology. I think you can't understand the world properly without knowing some science. Having a look in the museums will be a good way for me to improve my knowledge."

When they came abreast of the Natural History Museum Dan remarked, "Actually, just beyond the museums there's something else that I hope will add to your enjoyment of life in London: the Albert Hall. I've been going there ever since my father first took me when I was about eight years old. He's a great enthusiast for classical music. And of course there are several other places in town where you can hear great music."

"Maybe we could go to some of the concerts you call 'the Proms'? I've heard about them on television."

"That would be great. They start in July. I hope they're not sold out already. I'll try to get some tickets at the weekend, when you've had a look at the programme, and you can tell me which concerts take your fancy. Oh, dear. There always seems to be a traffic hold-up at this particular junction." The taxi had slowed to a halt in a line of cars and buses.

Dan went on, "I sometimes think it must be because of all the gullible tourists pouring out of Harrods with their purchases. I can't think why anyone would go there to do their shopping."

"You won't catch me there," said Gina, smiling. "Oh, we seem to be moving again."

They moved into Knightsbridge and were soon progressing along Piccadilly. As they passed the elegantly restrained façade of a large building on their left Dan remarked, "That's a club that has a peculiar name. It's called 'The In and Out' because of the signs on its two gateways. It's

161

actually the Naval and Military Club. My father and my Uncle Daniel are both members, and so I've had a number of good meals there over the years. Like most clubs it still has some antiquated practices. One part of the building is actually out of bounds to women."

"You mean the men's lavatories?" she asked, and they both burst into laughter.

When they reached Piccadilly Circus Gina said, "Now I do know where we are. If we had a puncture I think I could walk home from here."

"I don't think I'd want to carry the cases," said Dan, "though, of course, yours is on wheels. Actually, the taxi can't go by the shortest route because of the one-way system."

"Traffic in Rome was a nightmare," she said. "I hated driving there. I often used a taxi if the Metro wasn't convenient."

"I remember once attaching myself to a group of nuns when I was trying to get across the street near the Colosseum, in the hope that drivers might have some respect for them," said Dan.

"I'm glad you survived. I don't think Roman drivers respect anybody. The taxi-driver who took me to the station yesterday morning was complaining about the number of foreign tourists who bring their cars into Rome. He said they usually get lost and cause traffic jams – mainly French and Germans he thought. But I think the main problem is with the Romans themselves. I'm sure they've been doing it ever since they were running over people in their chariots."

There was another short traffic delay and then progress was steady. As they crossed over a four-way road junction Dan said, "Over there to the right is High Holborn, a street that has happy memories for me."

"The name sounds romantic but the buildings around here don't look very old," said Gina.

"They're not. In fact, some of them are very new. One of them is a rather ugly office building which stands on the site of what was once a pleasant little block of flats. That's where my unofficial uncle and aunt, Daniel and Ruth, used to live. When Daniel had to go off to the war in Korea

Ruth was there on her own and my parents often used to visit her, sometimes taking me with them. And later, when I was a teenager, I used to go there on my own. Ruth is a great baker and she makes delicious chocolate cake and great scones. Scones are very British – I'm sure she'll be happy to make some for you. Anyhow, some of my earliest memories are of my parents talking to her about Korea. She was very stoical; but then I think most people in her generation were."

"They needed to be," said Gina. "Maybe it was just because they'd been through so much that they didn't hesitate when they had to deal with Korea. Do you think our generation would be so resolute if they had to face up to something like that?"

"I hope enough of them would be. There'll always be some who find self-righteous reasons for not getting involved in what look like other people's problems. But Korea is the classic example of why it's vital not to hesitate. Just a few minutes ago I noticed that we passed a car that was made there, a Hyundai. When the war was over South Korea had been devastated by the Communist invasion, but it stayed open to the world and it recovered. Now it's one of the world's richer countries, even selling cars to Britain. The unfortunate North Koreans are still having trouble even feeding themselves adequately, although they seem to be good at making guns and bombs."

"Do you think maybe one day they'll get back their freedom like the East European countries are doing now?"

"I'm no expert on the Far East, but from what I've read it looks as if their Great Leader has an even tighter grip on power than Stalin had. My guess is that they'll be one of the last, but I hope they'll get there eventually."

When the taxi had crossed Southampton Row the driver asked, "What number is it in Lamb's Conduit Street, squire?" Dan told him the number but advised that he might find it easier to park a few yards farther along. And so it proved when they finally arrived.

When Dan had paid the driver, noticing as he did so that he was using the last of the sterling in his wallet, Gina said, "I'll take your little case and you can haul my big one up the stairs. I remember how steep they are." He was happy to accept the division of labour.

As he put his key into the door of the flat he said, "I'm afraid the place is in a bit of a mess. On Monday I had to leave in rather a hurry."

"I'm very good at tidying up," she said.

They put down the suitcases in the middle of the living-room. As he turned to face her Gina put her arms around his neck and said, "Thank you for bringing me back to my home. This time I'm here to stay."

And then she kissed him.

THE PEACEKEEPERS trilogy

This book is the third in the trilogy. The other two are also available from www.lulu.com and www.amazon.co.uk. (ISBN 978-0-9561569-1-4 and ISBN 978-0-9561569-2-1)

Following are extracts from the opening pages of the first two volumes:-

SLEEP QUIETLY IN YOUR BEDS

"That young Methodist minister was terrific, wasn't he? Do you think he was right when he said Europe is 'on the verge of a pacifist landslide'?" Ruth asked her friend, Nancy, as together they walked downstairs from the gallery of Westminster Central Hall in the midst of an elated throng of young Peace Pledge Union members. The Armistice Night meeting had been a rousing success and the speeches by the movement's famous leaders, some of whom she'd never actually seen before, were still reverberating in her head.

"He must have had some reason for thinking so. That German Roman Catholic, Solzbacher, seemed to think a lot of people in his church were coming round to the idea. Is that the first time you've heard Dr Soper? He is terrific, isn't he?" Nancy replied.

"Yes, it is. I wish I could go with you to one of his meetings on Tower Hill, but I'm always on duty at school on Wednesday lunchtimes. You're lucky that your office is so close"

They had reached the foyer and were preparing to go out into the November night when Ruth realized that her long, red woollen scarf was no longer in the pocket of her mackintosh. "Oh, crikey! I must have dropped my scarf. I'll have to fight my way back upstairs and see if I can find it."

"What rotten luck. I hope the mob haven't trampled it under foot," said Nancy. "I'll come and help you search for it."

They turned around and began to struggle upward against the descending flow of bodies. At the first landing Ruth suddenly caught a

165

glimpse of the red scarf being waved above heads to attract her attention, and a young man of about average height, wearing a grey trilby, edged his way through the flow towards her. "I saw it fall out of your pocket but I couldn't get to you because of all the people," he said, speaking with a slight, unfamiliar accent. "I was sure you'd notice it had gone once you got to the street."

DON'T LOSE IT AGAIN

The District Line train was full of people who were actually talking to each other in happy, excited voices when Ruth and Rebecca boarded it at Putney Bridge station. They managed to find enough space for their hands to clutch the central pole as the carriage jolted into motion.

"I can't remember when I last saw so many people travelling into town at this time of the day," said Ruth.

"Maybe, like us, they all waited at home to hear Mr Churchill on the wireless, and when that was over they set out to join in the celebrations," Rebecca observed.

"I hope they listened to what he said about this being just 'a brief period of rejoicing'. We've been given two days off, but after that it really is going to be back to – what did he call them? – 'toils and efforts that lie ahead'," said Ruth.

"Of course you are right about that, but we need to have the rejoicing, too. I think you English are not very good at that, but now is the time to do it and forget about everything else, just for a few hours."

Ruth looked at the unfamiliar smile on the usually serious face of her Jewish refugee friend and squeezed her arm. "You're absolutely right. If we can't be happy today we never will be; so let's enjoy it while we can. I hope we're going to be able to see Margarita when we get to Embankment. I asked her to wait for us just outside the Villiers Street entrance, but with so many people around it might not be easy for her; and she's not very tall."

"But I am, and I expect I'll be able to pick her out," said Rebecca. "It was very unselfish of her to volunteer to go into work this morning. She really seems to love her job."

"She does; but I wonder how much longer it's going to last, now," said Ruth. "I should think the BBC Monitoring Service will soon start cutting back on its Spanish language activities. They'll probably be spending all their resources on South-East Asia."

"Poor Margarita must have mixed feelings about today's celebrations," said Rebecca. "Her country is the one that hasn't got rid of its fascist dictator. Franco was very cunning, wasn't he, to keep Spain out of the war even when Hitler seemed to be winning?"

"Margarita was always hoping he would get involved, even though she knew it would make things more difficult for the Allies," Ruth replied.

Other novels by Derek Walker

(distribution at www.lulu.com and www.amazon.co.uk)

SENSE AND SENSUALITY

When Fatima, an asylum-seeker from Kazakhstan, meets Duncan Crauford she asks him to give her a bird's eye view of the history of Western civilization, to help her become British. Their quest takes them to the British Museum, the National Gallery and other sources of 'visual aids' in London. Meanwhile, Duncan, who is secretary-general of an international think-tank, is working with Paula, a Ugandan academic, on an analysis of the UN's failure to prevent genocide in Darfur. And his erotic friendship with Helen, a sensual university lecturer, is continuing even though she has decided to look for a husband, and thinks he isn't husband material. Her rejection makes him realize that he, too, is urgently in need of someone to share his bed; but he wonders what kind of woman could possibly be interested in a battle-scarred veteran like himself.

FOND DELUSIONS

In his final year at grammar school in Northern Ireland David Hunter's ambition is to work for peace in a world where the hydrogen bomb has just been invented. He wins a scholarship to the London School of Economics, and falls in love with a beautiful classmate. But when his love affair fails he joins the Foreign Legion, and takes part in the invasion of Suez. Returning injured to London he has an unexpected encounter that gives him new hope and a better understanding of the past.

MISRULE BRITANNIA

A journalist sent to cover a civil war in a former colony is plunged into the conflicts and corruption of an underdeveloped country. While the war escalates he falls in love with the woman of mixed race assigned to be his photographer. And when he gets close to the charismatic rebel leader he sees how personality can influence politics. The story sounds familiar, but the ex-colony is Britain and the journalist is Japanese – in an 'alternative history' scenario where eastern Asia takes on the historical role of western Europe. Looking at a world stage on which the actors have changed costumes may give the reader a new perspective on real events in recent decades. The pains and pleasures of the individual characters, however, could happen at any time, in any place.

A CASUAL CONQUEST

A young man from Japan starts his first job with the Honourable West Europa Company in Antwerp – in an 'alternative history' scenario in which Eighteenth Century Europe, having earlier been devastated by Mongol and Ottoman invasions, is reminiscent of South Asia in the dying years of the Mughal Empire. Before long he is listening to the Mozart Minstrels and is seduced by the Duchess of Holstein (who in 'real time' would have been Catherine the Great). Visiting Britain he sees a new altarpiece painted by Gainsborough and helps a young nun to escape to Antwerp. His bosses debate whether a trading company should take responsibility for governing failed states, and send him to observe a war in northern Germany between ambitious local rulers. He meets a famous native philosopher called 'Voltaire', and wonders if the British girl he left behind in Antwerp will welcome his return.

FAKING NEWS

When a minor news item on Radio 4 prompts Adam Turnbull to phone a friend he unwittingly takes the first step towards involvement in an international crisis. The action takes place a few years into the future, but underlying trends in politics and the media show few signs of change. Adam, an academic specialist in Balkan Studies, is sucked into ethnic cleansing, kidnapping and diplomatic deception, and he witnesses ways in which political, religious and NGO groups manipulate the media and are manipulated by them. His unwitting involvement in public events also brings him into intimate contact with two attractive women.

#0247 - 190916 - C0 - 234/156/9 - PB - DID1588004